ROBE

Roman... ...hin Man
and the Fat Lady

PENGUIN BOOKS

PENGUIN CLASSICS

Published by the Penguin Group
Penguin Books Ltd, 80 Strand, London WC2R 0RL, England
Penguin Group (USA), Inc., 375 Hudson Street, New York, New York 10014, USA
Penguin Group (Canada), 90 Eglinton Avenue East, Suite 700, Toronto, Ontario,
Canada M4P 2Y3 (a division of Pearson Penguin Canada Inc.)
Penguin Ireland, 25 St Stephen's Green, Dublin 2, Ireland (a division of Penguin Books Ltd)
Penguin Group (Australia), 250 Camberwell Road, Camberwell, Victoria 3124, Australia
(a division of Pearson Australia Group Pty Ltd)
Penguin Books India Pvt Ltd, 11 Community Centre, Panchsheel Park,
New Delhi – 110 017, India
Penguin Group (NZ), 67 Apollo Drive, Rosedale, North Shore 0632, New Zealand
(a division of Pearson New Zealand Ltd)
Penguin Books (South Africa) (Pty) Ltd, 24 Sturdee Avenue, Rosebank, Johannesburg 2196,
South Africa

Penguin Books Ltd, Registered Offices: 80 Strand, London WC2R 0RL, England

www.penguin.com

Selected from *Pricksongs and Descants*, published in the United States
by Grove Press 1969
This edition published in Penguin Classics 2011
3

Copyright © Robert Coover, 1969

Typeset by Jouve (UK), Milton Keynes
Printed in England by Clays Ltd, St Ives plc

ISBN: 978-0-141-19592-6

www.greenpenguin.co.uk

Contents

Romance of the Thin Man
and the Fat Lady

Now, many stories have been told, songs sung, about the Thin Man and the Fat Lady. Not only is there something comic in the coupling, but the tall erect and bony stature of the Man and the cloven mass of roseate flesh that is the Lady are in themselves metaphors too apparent to be missed. To be sure of it, one need only try to imagine a Thin Lady paired with a Fat Man. It is not ludicrous, it is unpleasant. No, the much recounted mating of the Thin Man with the Fat Lady is a circus legend full of truth. In fact, it is hardly more or less than the ultimate image of all our common everyday romances, which are also, let us confess, somehow comic. We are all Thin Men. You are all Fat Ladies.

But such simplicities are elusive; our metaphors turn on us, show us backsides human and complex. For observe them now: the Thin Man slumps soup-eyed and stoop-shouldered, seeming not thin so much as ill, and the Fat Lady in her stall sags immobile and turned blackly into herself. A passerby playfully punches his thumb into her thigh, an innocent commonplace event, and she spits in his eye.

'Hey, lady!'

'Right in his eye! I saw her!'

'What kinda circus is this, anyway?'

'She's probably not fat, just wearing a balloon suit!'

'Come, darling, don't get too close to the Fat Lady, something's wrong with her.'

Children cry, and lovers, strangely disturbed, turn quickly away from them, seeking out the monkey cage. Whoo! the Image of all our Romances indeed!

Yet perhaps – why yes! surely! – the signs are unmistakable: a third party has intruded.

Madame Cobra the Snakecharmer?

The Incredible Man with the Double Joints?

The Missing Link?

No, our triangle is of a more sinister genius. Our villain is the Ringmaster.

'We thought he'd understand. We were open about it. The circus life is a good life, but it's a tough one, too. A man's gotta be a man.'

'Get off that diet, Fat Lady, says he. The pig. Okay, okay, I say. But he doesn't believe me. He moves in on us! Can you imagine?'

'I was in the Strong Man's tent. I had twenty-five pounds up in the air, which for a Thin Man ain't bad. I'm pretty proud of it and when he comes in I say: Hey! look at that muscle! I'll show you muscle, says he, and kicks my poor ass all over that tent. He shouldn't do that. I got a very fragile spine.'

'Tape measure, calory charts, scales, everything. Don't take his beady eyes off us day or night. I ain't allowed to sweat, my Man can't exert hisself. What're we supposed to *do?*'

'Like animals, that's how he treats us. Livestock. Checks her teeth, hefts her udders, slaps her on the bare nates when she's on the scales. No heart at all. She's crying, but does he care? Eat! he says. Eat! You gotta let a woman be a woman, I believe that.'

It comes to this, then: that not even Ultimate Heroes are free from fashion. The Thin Man has wished to develop muscles, further to excite his Fat Lady –

'Builds stamina, too. Helps your wind.'

And the Lady has attempted to reduce to be more appealing to her Man –

'And I had my heart to think about. You understand.'

Now, were the Ringmaster a philosopher, he might have avoided the catastrophe – for, as in all true romances, and surely in the Truest, there is a catastrophe.

3

He might have been able to convince the couple with a merest syllogism of the absurdity – indeed the very contradiction! – of their respective wishes. But, far from being a philosopher, he indulges in the basest of trades (and is thus the best of villains!): he is a trafficker, a businessman, a financier, a Keeper of the Holier Books.

'Philosophy! You want philosophy? I'll give you philosophy! Okay, okay, so they're romantic symbols, I understand that, I'm not stupid, but what they symbolize, buddy, ain't Beauty. It's like that old fraud Merlin the Prestidigitator said when he came to try and soft-soap me: Who can blame them if they see outside themselves symbols of their own? There's something in all of us, Mr Ringmaster, he says, that rebels against extremes. Hell, I can follow that. And *being* a symbol: who wants it anyway? Narcissism, that's all it is. *But what the fuck else do you think a circus is all about?* Philosophy! Philosophy my ass! And the same goes for human nature! Want me to wreck my goddamn business? Listen! If the Fat Lady were not the fattest and the Thin Man the thinnest in the world – we're talking first principles now, buster – no one would pay to see them. Where are all your goddamn noble abstractions when the circus collapses and we're all of us out on the streets? *Adaptation*, boys and girls! *Expediency!* And to hell with nature!'

Things do not work out as well, however, as the Ringmaster has anticipated. The Fat Lady in her gloom loses her appetite and begins to waste away. The Thin Man stops eating altogether and must be held in an upright position all day by props. And even the Ringmaster, normally of such stable even if unpleasant temper, grows inexplicably fidgety in the long fumbling nights alongside the couple's troubled bed.

'She can't sleep, the poor dear. Whimpering all night long. I try to soothe her best I can, but my hands, so to speak, are tied.'

'One squeak of the bedsprings and on come the lights!'

'The man's a nut!'

'He looks down at my Man and says: That's one muscle too many! And throws cold water on it –'

'All night in a cold wet bed!'

At last, the Ringmaster negotiates a highly favorable contract of exchange with a rival circus, by which he is to acquire an Ambassador from Mars and a small sum of money for the waning Fat Lady. Another couple weeks, he thinks, and she would have been worthless. Hoo hee! a miraculous deal, a work of genius! Giggling softly (and no doubt meanly) to himself, he drops off that night into a comfortable slumber, the first in weeks, the bed beside him heaving fretfully the while with the parting anguish of the distraught lovers.

'It wasn't murder, it was a revolution.'

'A revolution of *love!*'

As one, the entire complement of the circus arises at midnight –

'Now!'

'Freedom!'

'Equality!'

'Clobber the fuckin lech!'

– summarily executes and inters the Ringmaster alongside the deserted country road (castrating him symbolically in the process – circus people are born to symbology!), and installs the Fat Lady and the Thin Man as Representative of the Common Proprietorship.

'We were all agreed. The Thin Man and the Fat Lady, in fact, were the last to know.'

'An Ambassador from Mars indeed! Did he think we had no pride?'

So joy reigns in the circus for weeks. Every performance concludes with a party. The two lovers' happiness seems to radiate magically, attracting new masses of spectators, all of which augments, in turn, their happiness. It is indeed a paradise. The Thin Man exercises without compunction and quickly reaps a sturdy little pair of biceps. The Fat Lady, all aglow, switches calory charts with the Thin Man, and within a week loses one of her several chins. Everyone, including the Thin Man, remarks on her beauty. Love is the word of the day. Circus people are basically good people. Their hatred for their former Ringmaster subsides, the souvenir taken from him is fed to the lions, and he is soon forgotten altogether. In a new day, there is no place for old resentments.

'I mean, you go along for years, see, thinking you got a Ringmaster on accounta you gotta have one. Ever seen a circus without a Ringmaster? No. Well, that just goes to show how history can fake you out!'

'It was beautiful! All of it just *happening!* Acts coming on spontaneously, here, there, it was wild and exciting and unpredictable!'

'Suddenly it hits you, see. All your life you been looking at circuses and you say, that's how circuses are. But what if they ain't? What if that's all a goddamn myth propagated by Ringmasters? You dig? What if it's all open-ended, and we can, if we want to, live by love?'

'We even started enjoying each other's acts!'

'I rode the elephant once!'

'Who says clowns gotta take pratfalls alla time? I learned to play in the band and train a bear and ride a horse through a fiery hoop!'

But, just when the picture is pinkest, bad news: it becomes all too apparent that fewer people are visiting the stalls of the Thin Man and the Fat Lady, and those that do pass through, do so hastily and with little interest.

'Okay, so they're happy, so they're in love. So what? You see one lover, you seen 'em all.'

At first, everyone stubbornly disregards the signs. The parties go on, the songs and the celebrations. The Thin Man lifts weights as always, and the Fat Lady diets. Their glad hearts, though gnawed at a bit by apprehension, remain kindled by love and joy. One could almost say it was the romantic legend come true. But finally they can no longer ignore the black-and-white truth of the circus ledger, now in their care. Somewhere, apparently, there is a fatter lady and a thinner man. Their new world threatens to crumble.

'We didn't wanna hurt their feelings, you know. We kidded them a little, hoping they'd take the hint.'

'Why couldn't they just love each other for themselves?'

'For the good of the whole circus, we said.'

In their van one night, doubt having doused for the moment the flame of passion, they agree: the Fat Lady will restore her castoff corpulence, the Thin Man will return his set of barbells to the Strong Man. They re-exchange calory charts. They begin in earnest to win back their public, found to be an integrant of their attachment, after all.

It is not easy. Worried by business reverses, the Fat Lady must work doubly hard to lay on each pound. And the Thin Man discovers that his little knots of muscle tend to sag instead of disappear. But they are driven by the most serious determination. The eyes of the circus are upon them. Momentary reverses only steel them more to the task.

'Chocolates! For me? It's been so long!'

'With love.'

'But now that you've seen me like this, will you truly love me when I'm fat again?'

'To be honest, dear, I ain't sure I can even tell the difference.'

The worst part of the day for the Fat Lady comes when she steps upon the scales. Disgusted by her fat, she is disgusted she has added so little of it. The Thin Man dutifully records her weight each day, and his presence comes to irritate her. He clucks his tongue when she fails to increase and sighs wistfully when she succeeds. She would cry but is afraid of the loss of anything, even tears. She refuses to submit to any activity which might make her perspire, and even demands that she be lifted in and out of the van each day.

The Thin Man steps daily before a full-length mirror. Disgusted by his thinness, he is disgusted that he still wears those little pouches under his skin. He wishes to be mere bone. Hilarious frightening unfleshed bone. The Fat Lady nags and pinches the little lumps that were once his muscles. He wonders if he has come to hate her.

'Hold up your arm there, loverboy, lemme feel that flab – hey! how cute! just like a little oyster!'

'Yeah? And so what?'

'So: oysters are a luxury, skinhead. People may pay to eat 'em, but they won't pay just to look!'

The Fat Lady, pointing out the Thin Man's bagginess, doubts he has been firm in his resolution, and snoops about for hidden food. The Man, grimly checking the Lady on the scales each day, begins to suspect her of burning off calories behind his back. They sneak into each other's stalls during the day, spy on one another at mealtimes, wrangle bitterly over the business books at night in their van. If one day the Fat Lady takes in a single dime more than the Thin Man, he must account for his obvious inconstancy of will. If a child carried past the Fat Lady's stall fails to laugh and point at her, the Thin Man uses it as proof of her deceptions. Of what use is she to the circus if not even a child is titillated? What is worse than a baggy Thin Man who can't make a dime?

'I'm sorry. I didn't build these goddamn biceps overnight, they don't shrink overnight neither. You can't exercise backwards, I tell her. You just go limp and hope for the best. But I do that and she just laughs at me. I think she's got her eye on Daredevil Dick.'

'Think of my nerves, I tell him. If they ain't fat nerves, he says, I got no use for them. All day, he's stuffing me. Even wants to add intravenous feedings. One day he brings home this dumbbell. He's got a mean glint in his eye – Nothing doing, I say. But it gives him this idea. Maybe you oughta get pregnant, he says. That'd work for nine months, I say, but then what? And he gives me this strange look.'

The situation deteriorates rapidly. The Thin Man becomes sour and morose, his shoulders stooped, head sunk in dark thoughts. The Fat Lady, immobile and glum, goes so far as to belch obscenely when a passerby remarks that she is really not so fat after all. They quarrel without cease, and their gloom spreads like wet sawdust through the whole circus. Gate receipts diminish and even the peanut sales drop off.

And then one night, the Thin Man moves abruptly to the old Ringmaster's van, something of a sacrifice on his part, since in the interim it has been used by a pair of camels. The Fat Lady bellows after him that she is glad to see him go (it's not true about Daredevil Dick, though: who could think about love in times like these?), as he stamps peevishly out of her van, the business books smuggled under his shirt. He renegotiates the old deal with the rival circus, and before anyone realizes what has happened, they have an Ambassador from Mars in their midst and the Fat Lady is gone. There are some unspecific rumbles of discontent, but since no one wishes to be sold to the rival circus, known to be on its last legs and infamous for its corrupt and tyrannical Ringmaster, these rumbles are held within discreet limits.

'Well, it was a crisis, after all. He did what he had to do. You had to think about the competition. They were all out to get us. It was the best thing for everybody.'

'She was my best friend. Everyone loved her. But no one seemed to care. I was alone. What could I say?'

'You get used to everything in this life.'

The Thin Man, in power, gains strength. He squares his shoulders and sets about getting the circus back on its feet. He is ruthless with himself as he has learned to be ruthless with others. The harder he works, the more rigorously he fasts. He *will* be thin, and damn the world! And even the unhappy Fat Lady, leagues distant, surrenders wearily to her fate and, doing so, finds it easy enough to expand once again.

But wait! See what we have come to! The Fat Lady separated from her inseparable Thin Man! The solution, for all the Thin Man's admirable will, cannot but fail. It is a circus without pleasure. What are three rings of determination? These are dismal shadowy tents and who can wander through their yawning flaps without a taste of dread? No, no, it is worse even than the mythological Thin Lady coupled with a Fat Man! Our metaphor, with time, has come unhinged! A rescue is called for!

Let us suppose, then, that the Thin Man is suddenly deposed, never mind why or how.

'Taking everything for himself.'

'Even started growing a moustache, bought himself a whip!'

'We had a meeting and –'

Never mind. The Ambassador from Mars, unexpectedly popular, assumes the Thin Man's functions, and the Man himself is exiled to the rival circus in exchange for a Family of Webfooted Midgets.

And so here we go! The Thin Man, all atremble and with tears springing to his eyes, here he comes, rushing pell mell into the Fat Lady's tent! All the circus people, the visiting crowds, the animals run behind, snorting, whooping, laughing giddily. Whoopee! into her arms! and she clasps him eagerly and forgivingly to her heaving bosom. Spectators weep for joy! The image is made whole!

'Beautiful! In spite of all history!'

'See how their joyful tears flow!'

'Oh! I'm all weepy and excited myself!'

'He buries his head in her lap!'

'Hold me!'

Later, when the world's love is momentarily spent and the crowds have slipped weakly away, she makes a space for him in her little van. It is rundown, like this whole decrepit circus, yet there is a corner in it still for happiness. This Ringmaster is, as all have rightly averred, a corrupt and mordant bastard, greedy beyond belief. But, by staying very fat and very thin, respectively, they satisfy his daytime proddings, and by night he is too absorbed in his ledgers to pay them notice.

Thus, though the sacrifices have been considerable, if indeed not prohibitive, we have obeyed the innocent bite in our forks and held fast to our precious metaphor.

Yet, somehow, strangely, it has lost some of its old charm. We go to the circus to see the Fat Lady and the Thin Man, and though warmed by them, perhaps even amused and incited by them still, we nevertheless return home somehow dissatisfied. Fat, yes, the Fattest, and Thin – but what is it? Maybe only that, as always, they are ludicrous, and that now, having gone to such lengths to reunite them, we are irritated to discover their limits, to find that the Ludicrous is not also Beautiful.

'Like, well, like they oughta do *more* for us some-how –'

'After all we've done for them!'

'Thin Man, Fat Lady, all right, it's cute, it's funny maybe, but . . .'

Well, let us admit it, perhaps it is ourselves who are corrupted. Perhaps we have seen or been too many Ring-masters, watched too many parades, safely witnessed too many thrills, counted through too many books. Maybe it's just that we've lost a taste for the simple in a world perplexingly simple. For, see, there? There a child laughs gaily at the Thin Man's tense smile, and there a young couple giggle in front of the unctuous Fat Lady.

So, what the hell, some circus music, please! Some raging lions and white horses and the clean cracking of black whips! Crackerjacks! Peanuts! And a monkey to wrap his tail around the flagpole!

For remember: these two, magic metaphor or no, are not the whole circus. Nor – to borrow from the hoariest spiel of them all – in this matter of circuses, is life one. There are three rings –

'Lazygentamun, absolutely unique, this way, patrons of the arts, desolate wastes, deepest Injah, suckled by werewolves, nekkid and hairy –'

'Raithiswhay, folks! She's half-human, half-reptile! Yawone believe yer eyes!'

'Absolutely wild gotta stand back limited time only, getcha tickets here, before goin inta the Big Top, see him now may never get another chance lives entirely on human flesh, ya heard me right, son! and we don't know how long we can keep him alive – !'

– And then there are more. Who can grasp it all? And who, grasping, can hold it! No, we have lost many things, go on losing, and must yet lose more. Even the Thin Man will grow old and bent, the Fat Lady will shrivel and die. We can hang on to nothing. Least of all the simple.

'This way, boyzungirls, inna the Big Show startin in jusfiminnit! still plennya seats but goodwonzur goin fast! yessir mistuh and how many – ?'

'Hey cottoncandy popcawn sodypop!'

'Getcha soovuhnih booklet while they last! Fittysens two quawtuhs of a dollah! Byootiful faw-color alla stars take a thrills home with ya!'

'There they come! It's the parade!'

'Lass chance now folks tellyawhawgawnuhdo! limited time only fore the Big Show gets unnerway! pay tenshun madam while supply lasts one quawtuh hurry! alla thrillsnchills Big Top in faw colors one quawtuh fifferadollah add extra bonus feachuh bagga nuts! you there – !'

But listen! the losses! these too are ludicrous, aren't

they? these too are part of the comedy, right? a ring around the rings! So, damn it, let us hoot and holler and thrill and eat peanuts and cheer and swill the pop and laugh and bawl! Come on! All us Thin Men! All you Fat Ladies!

'Annow lazygentamun anawyoo youngsters! (crack!) whatcha all been waiting for (crack!) inna the first ring feachuh act the Tumblin Twosome from Tuskyloosa (crack!) givum a hand folks! (crack!) inna second first time this side a the Atlantic comin to us from (crack!) and riding on a unicycle (crack!) whatsat rocket you carrying there George watchout! (crack!) and high above without a net those flirters with death (crack!) defying the lawza gravity (drumrolls and whipcracks!) you say it's a new secret weapon yer workin on for the guvmint George? well howzit work? (crack!) nothin but her teeth folks between her and the other world! (fanfare!) and his trained thoroughbred Arabian hawses! (crack!) now don't tell me you're gonna light that big thing in here George! (crack!) and rode by the Thin Man and the Fat Lady haw haw givum a big hand folks (crack!) *look out!*'

The Babysitter

She arrives at 7:40, ten minutes late, but the children, Jimmy and Bitsy, are still eating supper, and their parents are not ready to go yet. From other rooms come the sounds of a baby screaming, water running, a television musical (no words: probably a dance number – patterns of gliding figures come to mind). Mrs Tucker sweeps into the kitchen, fussing with her hair, and snatches a baby bottle full of milk out of a pan of warm water, rushes out again. 'Harry!' she calls. 'The babysitter's here already!'

That's My Desire? I'll Be Around? He smiles toothily, beckons faintly with his head, rubs his fast balding pate. Bewitched, maybe? Or, What's the Reason? He pulls on his shorts, gives his hips a slap. The baby goes silent in mid-scream. Isn't this the one who used their tub last time? Who's Sorry Now, that's it.

★

Jack is wandering around town, not knowing what to do. His girlfriend is babysitting at the Tuckers', and later, when she's got the kids in bed, maybe he'll drop over there. Sometimes he watches TV with her when she's babysitting, it's about the only chance he gets to make out a little since he doesn't own wheels, but they have to be careful because most people don't like their sitters to have boyfriends over. Just kissing her makes her nervous. She won't close her eyes because she has to be watching the door all the time. Married people really have it good, he thinks.

'Hi,' the babysitter says to the children, and puts her books on top of the refrigerator. 'What's for supper?' The little girl, Bitsy, only stares at her obliquely. She joins them at the end of the kitchen table. 'I don't have to go to bed until nine,' the boy announces flatly, and stuffs his mouth full of potato chips. The babysitter catches a glimpse of Mr Tucker hurrying out of the bathroom in his underwear.

Her tummy. Under her arms. And her feet. Those are the best places. She'll spank him, she says sometimes. Let her.

That sweet odor that girls have. The softness of her blouse. He catches a glimpse of the gentle shadows amid her thighs, as she curls her legs up under her. He stares hard at her. He has a lot of meaning packed into that stare, but she's not even looking. She's popping her gum and watching television. She's sitting right there, inches away, soft, fragrant, and ready: but what's his next move? He notices his buddy Mark in the drugstore, playing the pinball machine, and joins him. 'Hey, this mama's cold, Jack baby! She needs your touch!'

Mrs Tucker appears at the kitchen doorway, holding a rolled-up diaper. 'Now, don't just eat potato chips, Jimmy! See that he eats his hamburger, dear.' She hurries away to the bathroom. The boy glares sullenly at the babysitter, silently daring her to carry out the order. 'How about a little of that good hamburger now, Jimmy?' she says perfunctorily. He lets half of it drop to the floor. The baby is silent and a man is singing a love song on the TV. The children crunch chips.

He loves her. She loves him. They whirl airily, stirring a light breeze, through a magical landscape of rose and emerald and deep blue. Her light brown hair coils and wisps softly in the breeze, and the soft folds of her white gown tug at her body and then float away. He smiles in a pulsing crescendo of sincerity and song.

★

'You mean she's alone?' Mark asks. 'Well, there's two or three kids,' Jack says. He slides the coin in. There's a rumble of steel balls tumbling, lining up. He pushes a plunger with his thumb, and one ball pops up in place, hard and glittering with promise. His stare? to say he loves her. That he cares for her and would protect her, would shield her, if need be, with his own body. Grinning, he bends over the ball to take careful aim: he and Mark have studied this machine and have it figured out, but still it's not that easy to beat.

On the drive to the party, his mind is partly on the girl, partly on his own high-school days, long past. Sitting at the end of the kitchen table there with his children, she had seemed to be self-consciously arching her back, jutting her pert breasts, twitching her thighs: and for whom if not for him? So she'd seen him coming out of there, after all. He smiles. Yet what could he ever do about it? Those good times are gone, old man. He glances over at his wife, who, readjusting a garter, asks: 'What do you think of our babysitter?'

He loves her. She loves him. And then the babies come. And dirty diapers and one goddamn meal after another. Dishes. Noise. Clutter. And fat. Not just tight, her girdle actually hurts. Somewhere recently she's read about women getting heart attacks or cancer or something from too-tight girdles. Dolly pulls the car door shut with a grunt, strangely irritated, not knowing why. Party mood. Why is her husband humming, 'Who's Sorry Now?' Pulling out of the drive, she glances back at the lighted kitchen window. 'What do you think of our babysitter?' she asks. While her husband stumbles all over himself trying to answer, she pulls a stocking tight, biting deeper with the garters.

'Stop it!' she laughs. Bitsy is pulling on her skirt and he is tickling her in the ribs. 'Jimmy! Don't!' But she is laughing too much to stop him. He leaps on her, wrapping his legs around her waist, and they all fall to the carpet in front of the TV, where just now a man in a tuxedo and a little girl in a flouncy white dress are doing a tapdance together. The babysitter's blouse is pulling out of her skirt, showing a patch of bare tummy: the target. 'I'll spank!'

Jack pushes the plunger, thrusting up a steel ball, and bends studiously over the machine. 'You getting any off her?' Mark asks, and clears his throat, flicks ash from his cigarette. 'Well, not exactly, not yet,' Jack says, grinning awkwardly, but trying to suggest more than he admits to, and fires. He heaves his weight gently against the machine as the ball bounds off a rubber bumper. He can feel her warming up under his hands, the flippers suddenly coming alive, delicate rapid-fire patterns emerging in the flashing of the lights. 1000 WHEN LIT: *now!* 'Got my hand on it, that's about all.' Mark glances up from the machine, cigarette dangling from his lip. 'Maybe you need some help,' he suggests with a wry one-sided grin. 'Like maybe together, man, we could do it.'

She likes the big tub. She uses the Tuckers' bath salts, and loves to sink into the hot fragrant suds. She can stretch out, submerged, up to her chin. It gives her a good sleepy tingly feeling.

'What do you think of our babysitter?' Dolly asks, adjusting a garter. 'Oh, I hardly noticed,' he says. 'Cute girl. She seems to get along fine with the kids. Why?' 'I don't know.' His wife tugs her skirt down, glances at a lighted window they are passing, adding: 'I'm not sure I trust her completely, that's all. With the baby, I mean. She seems a little careless. And the other time, I'm almost sure she had a boyfriend over.' He grins, claps one hand on his wife's broad gartered thigh. 'What's wrong with that?' he asks. Still in anklets, too. Bare thighs, no girdles, nothing up there but a flimsy pair of panties and soft adolescent flesh. He's flooded with vague remembrances of football rallies and movie balconies.

How tiny and rubbery it is! she thinks, soaping between the boy's legs, giving him his bath. Just a funny jiggly little thing that looks like it shouldn't even be there at all. Is that what all the songs are about?

Jack watches Mark lunge and twist against the machine. Got her running now, racking them up. He's not too excited about the idea of Mark fooling around with his girlfriend, but Mark's a cooler operator than he is, and maybe, doing it together this once, he'd get over his own timidity. And if she didn't like it, there were other girls around. If Mark went too far, he could cut him off, too. He feels his shoulders tense: enough's enough, man . . . but sees the flesh, too. 'Maybe I'll call her later,' he says.

'Hey, Harry! Dolly! Glad you could make it!' 'I hope we're not late.' 'No, no, you're one of the first, come on in! By golly, Dolly, you're looking younger every day! How do you do it? Give my wife your secret, will you?' He pats her on her girdled bottom behind Mr Tucker's back, leads them in for drinks.

*

8:00. The babysitter runs water in the tub, combs her hair in front of the bathroom mirror. There's a western on television, so she lets Jimmy watch it while she gives Bitsy her bath. But Bitsy doesn't want a bath. She's angry and crying because she has to be first. The baby-sitter tells her if she'll take her bath quickly, she'll let her watch television while Jimmy takes his bath, but it does no good. The little girl fights to get out of the bathroom, and the babysitter has to squat with her back against the door and forcibly undress the child. There are better places to babysit. Both children mind badly, and then, sooner or later, the baby is sure to wake up for a diaper change and more bottle. The Tuckers do have a good color TV, though, and she hopes things will be settled down enough to catch the 8:30 program. She thrusts the child into the tub, but she's still screaming and thrashing around. 'Stop it now, Bitsy, or you'll wake the baby!' 'I have to go potty!' the child wails, switching tactics. The babysitter sighs, lifts the girl out of the tub and onto the toilet, getting her skirt and blouse all wet in the process. She glances at herself in the mirror. Before she knows it, the girl is off the seat and out of the bathroom. 'Bitsy! Come back here!'

'Okay, that's enough!' Her skirt is ripped and she's flushed and crying. 'Who says?' 'I do, man!' The bastard goes for her, but he tackles him. They roll and tumble. Tables tip, lights topple, the TV crashes to the floor. He slams a hard right to the guy's gut, clips his chin with a rolling left.

'We hope it's a girl.' That's hardly surprising, since they already have four boys. Dolly congratulates the woman like everybody else, but she doesn't envy her, not a bit. That's all she needs about now. She stares across the room at Harry, who is slapping backs and getting loud, as usual. He's spreading out through the middle, so why the hell does he have to complain about her all the time? 'Dolly, you're looking younger every day!' was the nice greeting she got tonight. 'What's your secret?' And Harry: 'It's all those calories. She's getting back her baby fat.' 'Haw haw! Harry, have a heart!'

'Get her feet!' he hollers at Bitsy, his fingers in her ribs, running over her naked tummy, tangling in the underbrush of straps and strange clothing. 'Get her shoes off!' He holds her pinned by pressing his head against her soft chest. 'No! No, Jimmy! Bitsy, stop!' But though she kicks and twists and rolls around, she doesn't get up, she can't get up, she's laughing too hard, and the shoes come off, and he grabs a stockinged foot and scratches the sole ruthlessly, and she raises up her legs, trying to pitch him off, she's wild, boy, but he hangs on, and she's laughing, and on the screen there's a rattle of hooves, and he and Bitsy are rolling around and around on the floor in a crazy rodeo of long bucking legs.

He slips the coin in. There's a metallic fall and a sharp click as the dial tone begins. 'I hope the Tuckers have gone,' he says. 'Don't worry, they're at our place,' Mark says. 'They're always the first ones to come and the last ones to go home. My old man's always bitching about them.' Jack laughs nervously and dials the number. 'Tell her we're coming over to protect her from getting raped,' Mark suggests, and lights a cigarette. Jack grins, leaning casually against the door jamb of the phonebooth, chewing gum, one hand in his pocket. He's really pretty uneasy, though. He has the feeling he's somehow messing up a good thing.

Bitsy runs naked into the livingroom, keeping a hassock between herself and the babysitter. 'Bitsy . . . !' the babysitter threatens. Artificial reds and greens and purples flicker over the child's wet body, as hooves clatter, guns crackle, and stagecoach wheels thunder over rutted terrain. 'Get outa the way, Bitsy!' the boy complains. 'I can't see!' Bitsy streaks past and the babysitter chases, cornering the girl in the back bedroom. Bitsy throws something that hits her softly in the face: a pair of men's undershorts. She grabs the girl scampering by, carries her struggling to the bathroom, and with a smart crack on her glistening bottom, pops her back into the tub. In spite, Bitsy peepees in the bathwater.

Mr Tucker stirs a little water into his bourbon and kids with his host and another man, just arrived, about their golf games. They set up a match for the weekend, a threesome looking for a fourth. Holding his drink in his right hand, Mr Tucker swings his left through the motion of a tee-shot. 'You'll have to give me a stroke a hole,' he says. 'I'll give you a stroke!' says his host: 'Bend over!' Laughing, the other man asks: 'Where's your boy Mark tonight?' 'I don't know,' replies the host, gathering up a trayful of drinks. Then he adds in a low growl: 'Out chasing tail probably.' They chuckle loosely at that, then shrug in commiseration and return to the livingroom to join their women.

Shades pulled. Door locked. Watching the TV. Under a blanket maybe. Yes, that's right, under a blanket. Her eyes close when he kisses her. Her breasts, under both their hands, are soft and yielding.

A hard blow to the belly. The face. The dark beardy one staggers. The lean-jawed sheriff moves in, but gets a spurred boot in his face. The dark one hurls himself forward, drives his shoulder into the sheriff's hard midriff, her own tummy tightens, withstands, as the sheriff smashes the dark man's nose, slams him up against a wall, slugs him again! and again! The dark man grunts rhythmically, backs off, then plunges suicidally forward – her own knees draw up protectively – the sheriff staggers! caught low! but instead of following through, the other man steps back – a pistol! the dark one has a pistol! the sheriff draws! shoots from the hip! explosions! she clutches her hands between her thighs – no! the sheriff spins! wounded! the dark man hesitates, aims, her legs stiffen toward the set, the sheriff rolls desperately in the straw, fires: dead! the dark man is dead! groans, crumples, his pistol drooping in his collapsing hand, dropping, he drops. The sheriff, spent, nicked, watches weakly from the floor where he lies. Oh, to be whole! to be good and strong and right! to embrace and be embraced by harmony and wholeness! The sheriff, drawing himself painfully up on one elbow, rubs his bruised mouth with the back of his other hand.

'Well, we just sorta thought we'd drop over,' he says, and winks broadly at Mark. 'Who's we?' 'Oh, me and Mark here.' 'Tell her, good thing like her, gotta pass it around,' whispers Mark, dragging on his smoke, then flicking the butt over under the pinball machine. 'What's that?' she asks. 'Oh, Mark and I were just saying, like two's company, three's an orgy,' Jack says, and winks again. She giggles. 'Oh, Jack!' Behind her, he can hear shouts and gunfire. 'Well, okay, for just a little while, if you'll both be good.' Way to go, man.

Probably some damn kid over there right now. Wrestling around on the couch in front of his TV. Maybe he should drop back to the house. Just to check. None of that stuff, she was there to do a job! Park the car a couple doors down, slip in the front door before she knows it. He sees the disarray of clothing, the young thighs exposed to the flickering television light, hears his baby crying. 'Hey, what's going on here! Get outa here, son, before I call the police!' Of course, they haven't really been doing anything. They probably don't even know how. He stares benignly down upon the girl, her skirt rumpled loosely around her thighs. Flushed, frightened, yet excited, she stares back at him. He smiles. His finger touches a knee, approaches the hem. Another couple arrives. Filling up here with people. He wouldn't be missed. Just slip out, stop back casually to pick up something or other he forgot, never mind what. He remembers that the other time they had this babysitter, she took a bath in their house. She had a date afterwards, and she'd just come from cheerleading practice or something. Aspirin maybe. Just drop quietly and casually into the bathroom to pick up some aspirin. 'Oh, excuse me, dear! I only . . . !' She gazes back at him, astonished, yet strangely moved. Her soft wet breasts rise and fall in the water, and her tummy looks pale and ripply. He recalls that her pubic hairs, left in the tub, were brown. Light brown.

She's no more than stepped into the tub for a quick bath, when Jimmy announces from outside the door that he has to go to the bathroom. She sighs: just an excuse, she knows. 'You'll have to wait.' The little nuisance. 'I can't wait.' 'Okay, then come ahead, but I'm taking a bath.' She supposes that will stop him, but it doesn't. In he comes. She slides down into the suds until she's eye-level with the edge of the tub. He hesitates. 'Go ahead, if you have to,' she says, a little awkwardly, 'but I'm not getting out.' 'Don't look,' he says. She: 'I will if I want to.'

She's crying. Mark is rubbing his jaw where he's just slugged him. A lamp lies shattered. 'Enough's enough, Mark! Now get outa here!' Her skirt is ripped to the waist, her bare hip bruised. Her panties lie on the floor like a broken balloon. Later, he'll wash her wounds, help her dress, he'll take care of her. Pity washes through him, giving him a sudden hard-on. Mark laughs at it, pointing. Jack crouches, waiting, ready for anything.

Laughing, they roll and tumble. Their little hands are all over her, digging and pinching. She struggles to her hands and knees, but Bitsy leaps astride her neck, bowing her head to the carpet. 'Spank her, Jimmy!' His swats sting: is her skirt up? The phone rings. 'The cavalry to the rescue!' she laughs, and throws them off to go answer.

Kissing Mark, her eyes closed, her hips nudge toward Jack. He stares at the TV screen, unsure of himself, one hand slipping cautiously under her skirt. Her hand touches his arm as though to resist, then brushes on by to rub his leg. This blanket they're under was a good idea. 'Hi! This is Jack!'

Bitsy's out and the water's running. 'Come on, Jimmy, your turn!' Last time, he told her he took his own baths, but she came in anyway. 'I'm not gonna take a bath,' he announces, eyes glued on the set. He readies for the struggle. 'But I've already run your water. Come on, Jimmy, please!' He shakes his head. She can't make him, he's sure he's as strong as she is. She sighs. 'Well, it's up to you. I'll use the water myself then,' she says. He waits until he's pretty sure she's not going to change her mind, then sneaks in and peeks through the keyhole in the bathroom door: just in time to see her big bottom as she bends over to stir in the bubblebath. Then she disappears. Trying to see as far down as the keyhole will allow, he bumps his head on the knob. 'Jimmy, is that you?' 'I – I have to go to the bathroom!' he stammers.

Not actually in the tub, just getting in. One foot on the mat, the other in the water. Bent over slightly, buttocks flexed, teats swaying, holding on to the edge of the tub. 'Oh, excuse me! I only wanted . . . !' He passes over her astonishment, the awkward excuses, moves quickly to the part where he reaches out to – 'What on earth are you doing, Harry?' his wife asks, staring at his hand. His host, passing, laughs. 'He's practicing his swing for Sunday, Dolly, but it's not going to do him a damn bit of good!' Mr Tucker laughs, sweeps his right hand on through the air as though lifting a seven-iron shot onto the green. He makes a *dok!* sound with his tongue. 'In there!'

'No, Jack, I don't think you'd better.' 'Well, we just called, we just, uh, thought we'd, you know, stop by for a minute, watch television for thirty minutes, or, or something.' 'Who's we?' 'Well, Mark's here, I'm with him, and he said he'd like to, you know, like if it's all right, just –' 'Well, it's *not* all right. The Tuckers said no.' 'Yeah, but if we only –' 'And they seemed awfully suspicious about last time.' 'Why? We didn't – I mean, I just thought –' 'No, Jack, and that's period.' She hangs up. She returns to the TV, but the commercial is on. Anyway, she's missed most of the show. She decides maybe she'll take a quick bath. Jack might come by anyway, it'd make her mad, that'd be the end as far as he was concerned, but if he should, she doesn't want to be all sweaty. And besides, she likes the big tub the Tuckers have.

He is self-conscious and stands with his back to her, his little neck flushed. It takes him forever to get started, and when it finally does come, it's just a tiny trickle. 'See, it was just an excuse,' she scolds, but she's giggling inwardly at the boy's embarrassment. 'You're just a nuisance, Jimmy.' At the door, his hand on the knob, he hesitates, staring timidly down on his shoes. 'Jimmy?' She peeks at him over the edge of the tub, trying to keep a straight face, as he sneaks a nervous glance back over his shoulder. 'As long as you bothered me,' she says, 'you might as well soap my back.'

'The aspirin . . .' They embrace. She huddles in his arms like a child. Lovingly, paternally, knowledgeably, he wraps her nakedness. How compact, how tight and small her body is! Kissing her ear, he stares down past her rump at the still clear water. 'I'll join you,' he whispers hoarsely.

She picks up the shorts Bitsy threw at her. Men's underwear. She holds them in front of her, looks at herself in the bedroom mirror. About twenty sizes too big for her, of course. She runs her hand inside the opening in front, pulls out her thumb. How funny it must feel!

'Well, man, I say we just go rape her,' Mark says flatly, and swings his weight against the pinball machine. 'Uff! Ahh! Get in there, you mother! Look at that! Hah! Man, I'm gonna turn this baby over!' Jack is embarrassed about the phone conversation. Mark just snorted in disgust when he hung up. He cracks down hard on his gum, angry that he's such a chicken. 'Well, I'm game if you are,' he says coldly.

8:30. 'Okay, come on, Jimmy, it's time.' He ignores her. The western gives way to a spy show. Bitsy, in pajamas, pads into the livingroom. 'No, Bitsy, it's time to go to bed.' 'You said I could watch!' the girl whines, and starts to throw another tantrum. 'But you were too slow and it's late. Jimmy, you get in that bathroom, and right now!' Jimmy stares sullenly at the set, unmoving. The babysitter tries to catch the opening scene of the television program so she can follow it later, since Jimmy gives himself his own baths. When the commercial interrupts, she turns off the sound, stands in front of the screen. 'Okay, into the tub, Jimmy Tucker, or I'll take you in there and give you your bath myself!' 'Just try it,' he says, 'and see what happens.'

They stand outside, in the dark, crouched in the bushes, peeking in. She's on the floor, playing with the kids. Too early. They seem to be tickling her. She gets to her hands and knees, but the little girl leaps on her head, pressing her face to the floor. There's an obvious target, and the little boy proceeds to beat on it. 'Hey, look at that kid go!' whispers Mark, laughing and snapping his fingers softly. Jack feels uneasy out here. Too many neighbors, too many cars going by, too many people in the world. That little boy in there is one up on him, though: he's never thought about tickling her as a starter.

His little hand, clutching the bar of soap, lathers shyly a narrow space between her shoulderblades. She is doubled forward against her knees, buried in rich suds, peeking at him over the edge of her shoulder. The soap slithers out of his grip and plunks into the water. 'I . . . I dropped the soap,' he whispers. She: 'Find it.'

'I dream of Jeannie with the light brown pubic hair!' 'Harry! Stop that! You're drunk!' But they're laughing, they're all laughing, damn! he's feeling pretty goddamn good at that, and now he just knows he needs that aspirin. Watching her there, her thighs spread for him, on the couch, in the tub, hell, on the kitchen table for that matter, he tees off on Number Nine, and – *whap*! – swats his host's wife on the bottom. 'Hole in one!' he shouts. 'Harry!' Why can't his goddamn wife Dolly ever get happy-drunk instead of sour-drunk all the time? 'Gonna be tough Sunday, old buddy!' 'You're pretty tough right now, Harry,' says his host.

The babysitter lunges forward, grabs the boy by the arms and hauls him off the couch, pulling two cushions with him, and drags him toward the bathroom. He lashes out, knocking over an endtable full of magazines and ashtrays. 'You leave my brother alone!' Bitsy cries and grabs the sitter around the waist. Jimmy jumps on her and down they all go. On the silent screen, there's a fade-in to a dark passageway in an old apartment building in some foreign country. She kicks out and somebody falls between her legs. Somebody else is sitting on her face. 'Jimmy! Stop that!' the babysitter laughs, her voice muffled.

She's watching television. All alone. It seems like a good time to go in. Just remember: really, no matter what she says, she wants it. They're standing in the bushes, trying to get up the nerve. 'We'll tell her to be good,' Mark whispers, 'and if she's not good, we'll spank her.' Jack giggles softly, but his knees are weak. She stands. They freeze. She looks right at them. 'She can't see us,' Mark whispers tensely. 'Is she coming out?' 'No,' says Mark, 'she's going into – that must be the bathroom!' Jack takes a deep breath, his heart pounding. 'Hey, is there a window back there?' Mark asks.

The phone rings. She leaves the tub, wrapped in a towel. Bitsy gives a tug on the towel. 'Hey, Jimmy, get the towel!' she squeals. 'Now stop that, Bitsy!' the babysitter hisses, but too late: with one hand on the phone, the other isn't enough to hang on to the towel. Her sudden nakedness awes them and it takes them a moment to remember about tickling her. By then, she's in the towel again. 'I hope you got a good look,' she says angrily. She feels chilled and oddly a little frightened. 'Hello?' No answer. She glances at the window – is somebody out there? Something, she saw something, and a rustling – footsteps?

'Okay, I don't care, Jimmy, don't take a bath,' she says irritably. Her blouse is pulled out and wrinkled, her hair is all mussed, and she feels sweaty. There's about a million things she'd rather be doing than babysitting with these two. Three: at least the baby's sleeping. She knocks on the overturned endtable for luck, rights it, replaces the magazines and ashtrays. The one thing that really makes her sick is a dirty diaper. 'Just go on to bed.' 'I don't have to go to bed until nine,' he reminds her. Really, she couldn't care less. She turns up the volume on the TV, settles down on the couch, poking her blouse back into her skirt, pushing her hair out of her eyes. Jimmy and Bitsy watch from the floor. Maybe, once they're in bed, she'll take a quick bath. She wishes Jack would come by. The man, no doubt the spy, is following a woman, but she doesn't know why. The woman passes another man. Something seems to happen, but it's not clear what. She's probably already missed too much. The phone rings.

Mark is kissing her. Jack is under the blanket, easing her panties down over her squirming hips. Her hand is in his pants, pulling it out, pulling it toward her, pulling it hard. She knew just where it was! Mark is stripping, too. God, it's really happening! he thinks with a kind of pious joy, and notices the open door. 'Hey! What's going on here?'

He soaps her back, smooth and slippery under his hand. She is doubled over, against her knees, between his legs. Her light brown hair, reaching to her gleaming shoulders, is wet at the edges. The soap slips, falls between his legs. He fishes for it, finds it, slips it behind him. 'Help me find it,' he whispers in her ear. 'Sure Harry,' says his host, going around behind him. 'What'd you lose?'

Soon be nine, time to pack the kids off to bed. She clears the table, dumps paper plates and leftover hamburgers into the garbage, puts glasses and silverware into the sink, and the mayonnaise, mustard, and ketchup in the refrigerator. Neither child has eaten much supper finally, mostly potato chips and ice cream, but it's really not her problem. She glances at the books on the refrigerator. Not much chance she'll get to them, she's already pretty worn out. Maybe she'd feel better if she had a quick bath. She runs water into the tub, tosses in bubblebath salts, undresses. Before pushing down her panties, she stares for a moment at the smooth silken panel across her tummy, fingers the place where the opening would be if there were one. Then she steps quickly out of them, feeling somehow ashamed, unhooks her brassiere. She weighs her breasts in the palms of her hands, watching herself in the bathroom mirror, where, in the open window behind her, she sees a face. She screams.

She screams: 'Jimmy! Give me that!' 'What's the matter?' asks Jack on the other end. 'Jimmy! Give me my towel! Right now!' 'Hello? Hey, are you still there?' 'I'm sorry, Jack,' she says, panting. 'You caught me in the tub. I'm just wrapped in a towel and these silly kids grabbed it away!' 'Gee, I wish I'd been there!' 'Jack – !' 'To protect you, I mean.' 'Oh, sure,' she says, giggling. 'Well, what do you think, can I come over and watch TV with you?' 'Well, not right this minute,' she says. He laughs lightly. He feels very cool. 'Jack?' 'Yeah?' 'Jack, I . . . I think there's somebody outside the window!'

She carries him, fighting all the way, to the tub, Bitsy pummeling her in the back and kicking her ankles. She can't hang on to him and undress him at the same time. 'I'll throw you in, clothes and all, Jimmy Tucker!' she gasps. 'You better not!' he cries. She sits on the toilet seat, locks her legs around him, whips his shirt up over his head before he knows what's happening. The pants are easier. Like all little boys his age, he has almost no hips at all. He hangs on desperately to his underpants, but when she succeeds in snapping these down out of his grip, too, he gives up, starts to bawl, and beats her wildly in the face with his fists. She ducks her head, laughing hysterically, oddly entranced by the spectacle of that pale little thing down there, bobbing and bouncing rubberily about with the boy's helpless fury and anguish.

'Aspirin? Whaddaya want aspirin for, Harry? I'm sure they got aspirin here, if you –' 'Did I say aspirin? I meant, uh, my glasses. And, you know, I thought, well, I'd sorta check to see if everything was okay at home.' Why the hell is it his mouth feels like it's got about six sets of teeth packed in there, and a tongue the size of that liverwurst his host's wife is passing around? 'Whaddaya want your glasses for, Harry? I don't understand you at all!' 'Aw, well, honey, I was feeling kind of dizzy or something, and I thought –' 'Dizzy is right. If you want to check on the kids, why don't you just call on the phone?'

They can tell she's naked and about to get into the tub, but the bathroom window is frosted glass, and they can't see anything clearly. 'I got an idea,' Mark whispers.

'One of us goes and calls her on the phone, and the other watches when she comes out.' 'Okay, but who calls?' 'Both of us, we'll do it twice. Or more.'

Down forbidden alleys. Into secret passageways. Unlocking the world's terrible secrets. Sudden shocks: a trapdoor! a fall! or the stunning report of a rifle shot, the *whaaii-ii-iing!* of the bullet biting concrete by your ear! Careful! Then edge forward once more, avoiding the light, inch at a time, now a quick dash for an open doorway – *look out!* there's a knife! a struggle! no! the long blade glistens! jerks! thrusts! *stabbed!* No, no, it missed! The assailant's down, yes! the spy's on top, pinning him, a terrific thrashing about, the spy rips off the assailant's mask: *a woman!*

Fumbling behind her, she finds it, wraps her hand around it, tugs. 'Oh!' she gasps, pulling her hand back quickly, her ears turning crimson. 'I . . . I thought it was the soap!' He squeezes her close between his thighs, pulls her back toward him, one hand sliding down her tummy between her legs. I Dream of Jeannie – 'I have to go to the bathroom!' says someone outside the door.

She's combing her hair in the bathroom when the phone rings. She hurries to answer it before it wakes the baby. 'Hello, Tuckers.' There's no answer. 'Hello?' A soft click. Strange. She feels suddenly alone in the big house, and goes in to watch TV with the children.

'Stop it!' she screams. 'Please, stop!' She's on her hands and knees, trying to get up, but they're too strong for her. Mark holds her head down. 'Now, baby, we're gonna teach you how to be a nice girl,' he says coldly, and nods at Jack. When she's doubled over like that, her skirt rides up her thighs to the leg bands of her panties. 'C'mon, man, go! This baby's cold! She needs your touch!'

Parks the car a couple blocks away. Slips up to the house, glances in his window. Just like he's expected. Her blouse is off and the kid's shirt is unbuttoned. He watches, while slowly, clumsily, childishly, they fumble with each other's clothes. My God, it takes them forever. 'Some party!' 'You said it!' When they're more or less naked, he walks in. 'Hey! What's going on here?' They go white as bleu cheese. Haw haw! 'What's the little thing you got sticking out there, boy?' 'Harry, behave yourself!' No, he doesn't let the kid get dressed, he sends him home bareassed. 'Bareassed!' He drinks to that. 'Promises, promises,' says his host's wife. 'I'll mail you your clothes, son!' He gazes down on the naked little girl on his couch. 'Looks like you and me, we got a little secret to keep, honey,' he says coolly. 'Less you wanna go home the same way your boyfriend did!' He chuckles at his easy wit, leans down over her, and unbuckles his belt. 'Might as well make it two secrets, right?' 'What in God's name are you talking about, Harry?' He staggers out of there, drink in hand, and goes to look for his car.

'Hey! What's going on here?' They huddle half-naked under the blanket, caught utterly unawares. On television: the clickety-click of frightened running feet on foreign pavements. Jack is fumbling for his shorts, tangled somehow around his ankles. The blanket is snatched away. 'On your feet there!' Mr Tucker, Mrs Tucker, Mark's mom and dad, the police, the neighbors, everybody comes crowding in. Hopelessly, he has a terrific erection. So hard it hurts. Everybody stares down at it.

Bitsy's sleeping on the floor. The babysitter is taking a bath. For more than an hour now, he's had to use the bathroom. He doesn't know how much longer he can wait. Finally, he goes to knock on the bathroom door. 'I have to use the bathroom.' 'Well, come ahead, if you have to.' 'Not while you're in there.' She sighs loudly. 'Okay, okay, just a minute,' she says, 'but you're a real nuisance, Jimmy!' He's holding on, pinching it as tight as he can. '*Hurry!*' He holds his breath, squeezing shut his eyes. No. Too late. At last, she opens the door. 'Jimmy!' 'I *told* you to hurry!' he sobs. She drags him into the bathroom and pulls his pants down.

He arrives just in time to see her emerge from the bathroom, wrapped in a towel, to answer the phone. His two kids sneak up behind her and pull the towel away. She's trying to hang onto the phone and get the towel back at the same time. It's quite a picture. She's got a sweet ass. Standing there in the bushes, pawing himself with one hand, he lifts his glass with the other and toasts her sweet ass, which his son now swats. Haw haw, maybe that boy's gonna shape up, after all.

They're in the bushes, arguing about their next move, when she comes out of the bathroom, wrapped in a towel. They can hear the baby crying. Then it stops. They see her running, naked, back to the bathroom like she's scared or something. 'I'm going in after her, man, whether you're with me or not!' Mark whispers, and he starts out of the bushes. But just then, a light comes sweeping up through the yard, as a car swings in the drive. They hit the dirt, hearts pounding. 'Is it the cops?' 'I don't know!' 'Do you think they saw us?' 'Sshh!' A man comes staggering up the walk from the drive, a drink in his hand, stumbles on in the kitchen door and then straight into the bathroom. 'It's Mr Tucker!' Mark whispers. A scream. 'Let's get outa here, man!'

9:00. Having missed most of the spy show anyway and having little else to do, the babysitter has washed the dishes and cleaned the kitchen up a little. The books on the refrigerator remind her of her better intentions, but she decides that first she'll see what's next on TV. In the livingroom, she finds little Bitsy sound asleep on the floor. She lifts her gently, carries her into her bed, and tucks her in. 'Okay, Jimmy, it's nine o'clock, I've let you stay up, now be a good boy.' Sullenly, his sleepy eyes glued still to the set, the boy backs out of the room toward his bedroom. A drama comes on. She switches channels. A ballgame and a murder mystery. She switches back to the drama. It's a love story of some kind. A man married to an aging invalid wife, but in love with a younger girl. 'Use the bathroom and brush your teeth before going to bed, Jimmy!' she calls, but as quickly regrets it, for she hears the baby stir in its crib.

Two of them are talking about mothers they've salted away in rest homes. Oh boy, that's just wonderful, this is one helluva party. She leaves them to use the john, takes advantage of the retreat to ease her girdle down awhile, get a few good deep breaths. She has this picture of her three kids carting her off to a rest home. In a wheelbarrow. That sure is something to look forward to, all right. When she pulls her girdle back up, she can't seem to squeeze into it. The host looks in. 'Hey, Dolly, are you all right?' 'Yeah, I just can't get into my damn girdle, that's all.' 'Here, let me help.'

She pulls them on, over her own, standing in front of the bedroom mirror, holding her skirt bundled up around the waist. About twenty sizes too big for her, of course. She pulls them tight from behind, runs her hand inside the opening in front, pulls out her thumb. 'And what a good boy am I!' She giggles: how funny it must feel! Then, in the mirror, she sees him: in the doorway behind her, sullenly watching. 'Jimmy! You're supposed to be in bed!' 'Those are my daddy's!' the boy says. 'I'm gonna tell!'

'Jimmy!' She drags him into the bathroom and pulls his pants down. 'Even your shoes are wet! Get them off!' She soaps up a warm washcloth she's had with her in the bathtub, scrubs him from the waist down with it. Bitsy stands in the doorway, staring. 'Get out! Get out!' the boy screams at his sister. 'Go back to bed, Bitsy. It's

49

just an accident.' 'Get out!' The baby wakes and starts to howl.

The young lover feels sorry for her rival, the invalid wife; she believes the man has a duty toward the poor woman and insists she is willing to wait. But the man argues that he also has a duty toward himself: his life, too, is short, and he could not love his wife now even were she well. He embraces the young girl feverishly; she twists away in anguish. The door opens. They stand there grinning, looking devilish, but pretty silly at the same time. 'Jack! I thought I told you not to come!' She's angry, but she's also glad in a way: she was beginning to feel a little too alone in the big house, with the children all sleeping. She should have taken that bath, after all. 'We just came by to see if you were being a good girl,' Jack says and blushes. The boys glance at each other nervously.

She's just sunk down into the tubful of warm fragrant suds, ready for a nice long soaking, when the phone rings. Wrapping a towel around her, she goes to answer: no one there. But now the baby's awake and bawling. She wonders if that's Jack bothering her all the time. If it is, brother, that's the end. Maybe it's the end anyway. She tries to calm the baby with the half-empty bottle, not wanting to change it until she's finished her bath. The bathroom's where the diapers go dirty, and they make it stink to high heaven. 'Shush, shush!' she whispers, rocking the crib. The towel slips away, leaving an airy empty tingle up and down her backside. Even before she stoops for the towel, even before she turns around, she knows there's somebody behind her.

'We just came by to see if you were being a good girl,' Jack says, grinning down at her. She's flushed and silent, her mouth half open. 'Lean over,' says Mark amiably. 'We'll soap your back, as long as we're here.' But she just huddles there, down in the suds, staring up at them with big eyes.

'Hey! What's going on here?' It's Mr Tucker, stumbling through the door with a drink in his hand. She looks up from the TV. 'What's the matter, Mr Tucker?' 'Oh, uh, I'm sorry, I got lost – no, I mean, I had to get some aspirin. Excuse me!' And he rushes past her into the bathroom, caroming off the livingroom door jamb on the way. The baby wakes.

'Okay, get off her, Mr Tucker!' 'Jack!' she cries, 'what are *you* doing here?' He stares hard at them a moment: so that's where it goes. Then, as Mr Tucker swings heavily off, he leans into the bastard with a hard right to the belly. Next thing he knows, though, he's got a face full of an old man's fist. He's not sure, as the lights go out, if that's his girlfriend screaming or the baby . . .

Her host pushes down on her fat fanny and tugs with all his might on her girdle, while she bawls on his shoulder: 'I don't *wanna* go to a rest home!' 'Now, now, take it easy, Dolly, nobody's gonna make you –' 'Ouch! Hey, you're hurting!' 'You should buy a bigger girdle, Dolly.' 'You're telling me?' Some other guy pokes his head in. 'Whatsamatter? Dolly fall in?' 'No, she fell out. Give me a hand.'

By the time she's chased Jack and Mark out of there, she's lost track of the program she's been watching on television. There's another woman in the story now for some reason. That guy lives a very complicated life. Impatiently, she switches channels. She hates ballgames, so she settles for the murder mystery. She switches just in time, too: there's a dead man sprawled out on the floor of what looks like an office or a study or something. A heavyset detective gazes up from his crouch over the body: 'He's been strangled.' Maybe she'll take that bath, after all.

She drags him into the bathroom and pulls his pants down. She soaps up a warm washcloth she's had in the tub with her, but just as she reaches between his legs, it starts to spurt, spraying her arms and hands. 'Oh, Jimmy! I thought you were done!' she cries, pulling him toward the toilet and aiming it into the bowl. How moist and rubbery it is! And you can turn it every which way. How funny it must feel!

'Stop it!' she screams. 'Please stop!' She's on her hands and knees and Jack is holding her head down. 'Now we're gonna teach you how to be a nice girl,' Mark says and lifts her skirt. 'Well, I'll be damned!' 'What's the matter?' asks Jack, his heart pounding. 'Look at this big pair of men's underpants she's got on!' 'Those are my daddy's!' says Jimmy, watching them from the doorway. 'I'm gonna tell!'

People are shooting at each other in the murder mystery, but she's so mixed up, she doesn't know which ones are the good guys. She switches back to the love story. Something seems to have happened, because now the man is kissing his invalid wife tenderly. Maybe she's finally dying. The baby wakes, begins to scream. Let it. She turns up the volume on the TV.

Leaning down over her, unbuckling his belt. It's all happening just like he's known it would. Beautiful! The kid is gone, though his pants, poor lad, remain. 'Looks like you and me, we got a secret to keep, child!' But he's cramped on the couch and everything is too slippery and small. 'Lift your legs up, honey. Put them around my back.' But instead, she screams. He rolls off, crashing to the floor. There they all come, through the front door. On television, somebody is saying: 'Am I a burden to you, darling?' 'Dolly! My God! Dolly, I can explain . . . !'

The game of the night is Get Dolly Tucker Back in Her Girdle Again. They've got her down on her belly in the livingroom and the whole damn crowd is working on her. Several of them are stretching the girdle, while others try to jam the fat inside. 'I think we made a couple inches on this side! Roll her over!' Harry?

She's just stepped into the tub, when the phone rings, waking the baby. She sinks down in the suds, trying not to hear. But that baby doesn't cry, it screams. Angrily, she wraps a towel around herself, stamps peevishly into the baby's room, just letting the phone jangle. She tosses the baby down on its back, unpins its diapers hastily, and gets yellowish baby stool all over her hands. Her towel drops away. She turns to find Jimmy staring at her like a little idiot. She slaps him in the face with her dirty hand, while the baby screams, the phone rings, and nagging voices argue on the TV. There are better things she might be doing.

What's happening? Now there's a young guy in it. Is he after the young girl or the old invalid? To tell the truth, it looks like he's after the same man the women are. In disgust, she switches channels. 'The strangler again,' growls the fat detective, hands on hips, staring down at the body of a half-naked girl. She's considering either switching back to the love story or taking a quick bath, when a hand suddenly clutches her mouth.

'You're both chicken,' she says, staring up at them. 'But what if Mr Tucker comes home?' Mark asks nervously.

How did he get here? He's standing pissing in his own goddamn bathroom, his wife is still back at the party, the three of them are, like good kids, sitting in there in the livingroom watching TV. One of them is his host's boy Mark. 'It's a good murder mystery, Mr Tucker,' Mark said, when he came staggering in on them a minute ago. 'Sit still!' he shouted, 'I'm just home for a moment!' Then whump thump on into the bathroom. Long hike for a weewee, Mister. But something keeps bothering him. Then it hits him: the girl's panties, hanging like a broken balloon from the rabbit-ear antennae

55

on the TV! He barges back in there, giving his shoulder a helluva crack on the livingroom door jamb on the way – but they're not hanging there any more. Maybe he's only imagined it. 'Hey, Mr Tucker,' Mark says flatly. 'Your fly's open.'

The baby's dirty. Stinks to high heaven. She hurries back to the livingroom, hearing sirens and gunshots. The detective is crouched outside a house, peering in. Already, she's completely lost. The baby screams at the top of its lungs. She turns up the volume. But it's all confused. She hurries back in there, claps an angry hand to the baby's mouth. 'Shut up!' she cries. She throws the baby down on its back, starts to unpin the diaper, as the baby tunes up again. The phone rings. She answers it, one eye on the TV. '*What?*' The baby cries so hard it starts to choke. Let it. 'I said, hi, this is Jack!' Then it hits her: oh no! the diaper pin!

'The aspirin . . .' But she's already in the tub. Way down in the tub. Staring at him through the water. Her tummy looks pale and ripply. He hears sirens, people on the porch.

Jimmy gets up to go to the bathroom and gets his face slapped and smeared with baby poop. Then she hauls him off to the bathroom, yanks off his pajamas, and throws him into the tub. That's okay, but next she gets naked and acts like she's gonna get in the tub, too. The baby's screaming and the phone's ringing like crazy and in walks his dad. Saved! he thinks, but, no, his dad grabs him right back out of the tub and whales the dickens out of him, no questions asked, while she watches, then sends him – *whack!* – back to bed. So he's lying there, wet and dirty and naked and sore, and he still has to go to the bathroom, and outside his window he hears two older guys talking. 'Listen, you know where to do it if we get her pinned?' 'No! Don't you?'

'Yo ho heave ho! *Ugh!*' Dolly's on her back and they're working on the belly side. Somebody got the great idea of buttering her down first. Not to lose the ground they've gained, they've shot it inside with a basting syringe. But now suddenly there's this big tug-of-war under way between those who want to stuff her in and those who want to let her out. Something rips, but she feels better. The odor of hot butter makes her think of movie theaters and popcorn. 'Hey, has anybody seen Harry?' she asks. 'Where's Harry?'

Somebody's getting chased. She switches back to the love story, and now the man's back kissing the young lover again. What's going on? She gives it up, decides to take a quick bath. She's just stepping into the tub, one foot in, one foot out, when Mr Tucker walks in. 'Oh, excuse me! I only wanted some aspirin . . .' She grabs for a towel, but he yanks it away. 'Now, that's not how it's supposed to happen, child,' he scolds. 'Please! Mr Tucker . . . !' He embraces her savagely, his calloused old hands clutching roughly at her backside. 'Mr Tucker!' she cries, squirming. 'Your wife called – !' He's pushing something between her legs, hurting her. She slips, they both slip – something cold and hard slams her in the back, cracks her skull, she seems to be sinking into a sea . . .

They've got her over the hassock, skirt up and pants down. 'Give her a little lesson there, Jack baby!' The television lights flicker and flash over her glossy flesh. 1000 WHEN LIT. Whack! Slap! Bumper to bumper! He leans into her, feeling her come alive.

The phone rings, waking the baby. 'Jack, is that you? Now, you listen to me – !' 'No, dear, this is Mrs Tucker. Isn't the TV awfully loud?' 'Oh, I'm sorry, Mrs Tucker! I've been getting –' 'I tried to call you before, but I couldn't hang on. To the phone, I mean. I'm sorry, dear.' 'Just a minute, Mrs Tucker, the baby's –' 'Honey, listen! Is Harry there? Is Mr Tucker there, dear?'

★

'Stop it!' she screams and claps a hand over the baby's mouth. 'Stop it! Stop it! *Stop it!*' Her other hand is full of baby stool and she's afraid she's going to be sick. The phone rings. 'No!' she cries. She's hanging on to the baby, leaning woozily away, listening to the phone ring. 'Okay, okay,' she sighs, getting ahold of herself. But when she lets go of the baby, it isn't screaming any more. She shakes it. Oh no . . .

'Hello?' No answer. Strange. She hangs up and, wrapped only in a towel, stares out the window at the cold face staring in – she screams!

She screams, scaring the hell out of him. He leaps out of the tub, glances up at the window she's gaping at just in time to see two faces duck away, then slips on the bathroom tiles, and crashes to his ass, whacking his head on the sink on the way down. She stares down at him, trembling, a towel over her narrow shoulders. 'Mr Tucker! Mr Tucker, are you all right . . .?' Who's Sorry Now? Yessir, who's back is breaking with each . . . He stares up at the little tufted locus of all his woes, and passes out, dreaming of Jeannie . . .

The phone rings. 'Dolly! It's for you!' 'Hello?' 'Hello, Mrs Tucker?' 'Yes, speaking.' 'Mrs Tucker, this is the police calling . . .'

*

It's cramped and awkward and slippery, but he's pretty sure he got it in her, once anyway. When he gets the suds out of his eyes, he sees her staring up at them. Through the water. 'Hey, Mark! Let her up!'

Down in the suds. Feeling sleepy. The phone rings, startling her. Wrapped in a towel, she goes to answer. 'No, he's not here, Mrs Tucker.' Strange. Married people act pretty funny sometimes. The baby is awake and screaming. Dirty, a real mess. Oh boy, there's a lot of things she'd rather be doing than babysitting in this madhouse. She decides to wash the baby off in her own bathwater. She removes her towel, unplugs the tub, lowers the water level so the baby can sit. Glancing back over her shoulder, she sees Jimmy staring at her. 'Go back to bed, Jimmy.' 'I have to go to the bathroom.' 'Good grief, Jimmy! It looks like you already have!' The phone rings. She doesn't bother with the towel – what can Jimmy see he hasn't already seen? – and goes to answer. 'No, Jack, and that's final.' Sirens, on the TV, as the police move in. But wasn't that the channel with the love story? Ambulance maybe. Get this over with so she can at least catch the news. 'Get those wet pajamas off, Jimmy, and I'll find clean ones. Maybe you better get in the tub, too.' 'I think something's wrong with the baby,' he says. 'It's down in the water and it's not swimming or anything.'

She's staring up at them from the rug. They slap her. Nothing happens. 'You just tilted her, man!' Mark says softly. 'We gotta get outa here!' Two little kids are standing wide-eyed in the doorway. Mark looks hard at Jack. 'No, Mark, they're just little kids . . . !' 'We gotta, man, or we're dead.'

'Dolly! My God! Dolly, I can explain!' She glowers down at them, her ripped girdle around her ankles. 'What the four of you are doing in the bathtub with *my* babysitter?' she says sourly. 'I can hardly wait!'

Police sirens wail, lights flash. 'I heard the scream!' somebody shouts. 'There were two boys!' 'I saw a man!' 'She was running with the baby!' 'My God!' somebody screams, 'they're *all* dead!' Crowds come running. Spotlights probe the bushes.

'Harry, where the hell you been?' his wife whines, glaring blearily up at him from the carpet. 'I can explain,' he says. 'Hey, whatsamatter, Harry?' his host asks, smeared with butter for some goddamn reason. 'You look like

61

you just seen a ghost!' Where did he leave his drink? Everybody's laughing, everybody except Dolly, whose cheeks are streaked with tears. 'Hey, Harry, you won't let them take me to a rest home, will you, Harry?'

10:00. The dishes done, children to bed, her books read, she watches the news on television. Sleepy. The man's voice is gentle, soothing. She dozes – awakes with a start: a babysitter? Did the announcer say something about a babysitter?

'Just want to catch the weather,' the host says, switching on the TV. Most of the guests are leaving, but the Tuckers stay to watch the news. As it comes on, the announcer is saying something about a babysitter. The host switches channels. 'They got a better weatherman on four,' he explains. 'Wait!' says Mrs Tucker. 'There was something about a babysitter . . . !' The host switches back. 'Details have not yet been released by the police,' the announcer says. 'Harry, maybe we'd better go . . .'

They stroll casually out of the drugstore, run into a buddy of theirs. 'Hey! Did you hear about the baby-sitter?' the guy asks. Mark grunts, glances at Jack. 'Got a smoke?' he asks the guy.

★

'I think I hear the baby screaming!' Mrs Tucker cries, running across the lawn from the drive.

She wakes, startled, to find Mr Tucker hovering over her. 'I must have dozed off!' she exclaims. 'Did you hear the news about the babysitter?' Mrs Tucker asks. 'Part of it,' she says, rising. 'Too bad, wasn't it?' Mr Tucker is watching the report of the ball scores and golf tournaments. 'I'll drive you home in just a minute, dear,' he says. 'Why, how nice!' Mrs Tucker exclaims from the kitchen. 'The dishes are all done!'

'What can I say, Dolly?' the host says with a sigh, twisting the buttered strands of her ripped girdle between his fingers. 'Your children are murdered, your husband gone, a corpse in your bathtub, and your house is wrecked. I'm sorry. But what can I say?' On the TV, the news is over, and they're selling aspirin. 'Hell, *I* don't know,' she says. 'Let's see what's on the late late movie.'

A Pedestrian Accident

Paul stepped off the curb and got hit by a truck. He didn't know what it was that hit him at first, but now, here on his back, under the truck, there could be no doubt. Is it me? he wondered. Have I walked the earth and come here?

Just as he was struck, and while still tumbling in front of the truck and then under the wheels, in a kind of funhouse gambado of pain and terror, he had thought: this has happened before. His neck had sprung, there was a sudden flash of light and a blaze roaring up in the back of his head. The hot – almost fragrant – pain: that was new. It was the *place* he felt he'd returned to.

He lay perpendicular to the length of the truck, under the trailer, just to the rear of the truck's second of three sets of wheels. All of him was under the truck but his head and shoulders. Maybe I'm being born again, he reasoned. He stared straight up, past the side of the truck, toward the sky, pale blue and cloudless. The tops of skyscrapers closed toward the center of his vision; now that he thought about it, he realized it was the first time in years he had looked up at them, and they seemed inclined to fall. The old illusion; one of them anyway. The truck was red with white letters, but his severe angle of vision up the side kept him from being able to read the letters. A capital 'K,' he could see that – and a number, yes, it seemed to be a '14.' He smiled inwardly at the irony, for he had a private fascination with numbers: fourteen! He thought he remembered having had a green light, but it didn't really matter. No way to prove it. It would have changed by now, in any case. The thought, obscurely, troubled him.

'Crazy goddamn fool he just walk right out in fronta me no respect just burstin for a bustin!'

The voice, familiar somehow, guttural, yet falsetto, came from above and to his right. People were gathering to stare down at him, shaking their heads. He felt like one chosen. He tried to turn his head toward the voice, but his neck flashed hot again. Things were bad. Better just to lie still, take no chances. Anyway, he saw now, just in the corner of his eye, the cab of the truck, red like the trailer, and poking out its window, the large head of the truckdriver, wagging in the sunshine. The driver wore a small tweed cap – too small, in fact: it sat just on top of his head.

'Boy I seen punchies in my sweet time but this cookie

takes the cake God bless the laboring classes I say and preserve us from the humble freak!'

The truckdriver spoke with broad gestures, bulbous eyes rolling, runty body thrusting itself in and out of the cab window, little hands flying wildly about. Paul worried still about the light. It was important, yet how could he ever know? The world was an ephemeral place, it could get away from you in a minute. The driver had a bent red nose and coarse reddish hair that stuck out like straw. A hard shiny chin, too, like a mirror image of the hooked nose. Paul's eyes wearied of the strain, and he had to stop looking.

'Listen lays and gentmens I'm a good Christian by Judy a decent hardworkin fambly man earnin a honest wage and got a dear little woman and seven yearnin younguns all my own seed *a responsible man* and goddamn that boy what he do but walk right into me and my poor ole truck!'

On some faces Paul saw compassion, or at least a neutral curiosity, an idle amusement, but on most he saw reproach. There were those who winced on witnessing his state and seemed to understand, but there were others – a majority – who jeered.

'He asked for it if you ask me!'

'It's the idler plays the fool and the workingman's to hang for it!'

'Shouldn't allow his kind out to walk the streets!'

'What is the use of running when you are on the wrong road?'

It worsened. Their shouts grew louder and ran together. There were orations and the waving of flags. Paul was wondering: had he been carrying anything? No, no. He had only – *wait!* a book? Very likely, but . . . ah well. Perhaps he was carrying it still. There was no feeling in his fingers.

The people were around him like flies, grievances were being aired, sides taken, and there might have been a brawl, but a policeman arrived and broke it up. 'All right, everybody! Stand back, please!' he shouted. 'Give this man some air! Can't you see he's been injured?'

At last, Paul thought. He relaxed. For a moment, he'd felt himself in a strange and hostile country, but now he felt at home again. He even began to believe he might survive. Though really: had he ever doubted it?

'Everybody back, *back!*' The policeman was effective. The crowd grew quiet, and by the sound of their sullen shuffling, Paul guessed they were backing off. Not that he got more or less air by it, but he felt relieved just the same. 'Now,' said the policeman, gently but firmly, 'what has happened here?'

And with that it all started up again, same as before,

the clamor, the outrage, the arguments, the learned quotations, but louder and more discordant than ever. I'm hurt, Paul said. No one heard. The policeman cried out for order, and slowly, with his shouts, with his night-stick, with his threats, he reduced them again to silence.

One lone voice hung at the end: ' – for the last time, Mister, *stop goosing me!*' Everybody laughed, released.

'Stop goosing her, sir!' the policeman commanded with his chin thrust firmly forward, and everybody laughed again.

Paul almost laughed, but he couldn't, quite. Besides, he'd just, with that, got the picture, and given his condition, it was not a funny one. He opened his eyes and there was the policeman bent down over him. He had a notebook in his hand.

'Now, tell me, son, what happened here?' The police-man's face was thin and pale, like a student's, and he wore a trim little tuft of black moustache under the pinched peak of his nose.

I've just been hit, Paul explained, by this truck, and then he realized that he probably didn't say it at all, that speech was an art no longer his. He cast his eyes indica-tively toward the cab of the truck.

'Listen, I asked you what happened here! Cat got your tongue, young man?'

'Crazy goddam fool he just walk right out in fronta me no respect just burstin for a bustin!'

The policeman remained crouched over Paul, but turned his head up to look at the truckdriver. The policeman wore a brilliant blue uniform with large brass buttons. And gold epaulettes.

'Boy I seen punchies in my sweet time but this cookie takes the cake God bless the laboring classes I say and preserve us from the humble freak!'

The policeman looked down at Paul, then back at the truckdriver. 'I know about truckdrivers,' Paul heard him say.

'Listen lays and gentmens I'm a good Christian by Judy a decent hardworkin fambly man earnin a honest wage and got a dear little woman and seven yearnin younguns all my own seed *a responsible man* and goddamn that boy what he do but walk right into me and my poor ole trike. Truck, I mean.'

There was a loose tittering from the crowd, but the policeman's frown and raised stick contained it. 'What's your name, lad?' he asked, turning back to Paul. At first, the policeman smiled, he knew who truckdrivers were and he knew who Pauls were, and there was a salvation of sorts in that smile, but gradually it faded. 'Come, come, boy! Don't be afraid!' He winked, nudged him gently. 'We're here to help you.'

Paul, Paul replied. But, no, no doubt about it, it was jammed up in there and he wasn't getting it out.

'Well, if you won't help me, I can't help you,' the policeman said pettishly and tilted his nose up. 'Anybody here know this man?' he called out to the crowd.

Again a roar, a threatening tumult of words and sounds, shouts back and forth. It was hard to know if none knew him or if they all did. But then one voice, belted out above the others, came through: 'O God in heaven! It's Amory! *Amory Westerman!*' The voice, a woman's, hysterical by the sound of it, drew near. 'Amory! What . . . *what* have they *done* to you?'

Paul understood. It was not a mistake. He was astonished by his own acumen.

'Do you know this young man?' the policeman asked, lifting his notebook.

'What? Know him? Did Sarah know Abraham? Did Eve know Cain?'

The policeman cleared his throat uneasily. 'Adam,' he corrected softly.

'You know who you know, I know who I know,' the woman said, and let fly with a low throaty snigger. The crowd responded with a belly laugh.

'But this young man – !' the policeman insisted, flustered.

'Who, you and Amory?' the woman cried. 'I can't

believe it!' The crowd laughed and the policeman bit his lip. 'Amory! What new persecutions are these?' She billowed out above him: old, maybe even seventy, fat and bosomy, pasty-faced with thick red rouges, head haloed by ringlets of sparse orangish hair. 'My poor Amory!' And down she came on him. Paul tried to duck, got only a hot flash in his neck for it. Her breath reeked of cheap gin. Help, said Paul.

'Hold, madame! Stop!' the policeman cried, tugging at the woman's sleeve. She stood, threw up her arms before her face, staggered backwards. What more she did, Paul couldn't see, for his view of her face was largely blocked by the bulge of her breasts and belly. There were laughs, though. 'Everything in order here,' grumped the policeman, tapping his notebook. 'Now, what's your name, please . . . uh . . . miss, madame?'

'My name?' She twirled gracelessly on one dropsied ankle and cried to the crowd: *'Shall I tell?'*

'Tell! Tell! Tell!' shouted the spectators, clapping rhythmically. Paul let himself be absorbed by it; there was, after all, nothing else to do.

The policeman, rapping a pencil against his blue notebook to the rhythm of the chant, leaned down over Paul and whispered: ('I think we've got them on our side now!')

Paul, his gaze floating giddily up past the thin white

face of the police officer and the red side of the truck into the horizonless blue haze above, wondered if alliance were really the key to it all. What *am* I without them? Could I even die? Suddenly, the whole world seemed to tip: his feet dropped and his head rose. Beneath him the red machine shot grease and muck, the host rioted above his head, the earth pushed him from behind, and out front the skyscrapers pointed, like so many insensate fingers, the path he must walk to oblivion. He squeezed shut his eyes to set right the world again – he was afraid he would slide down beneath the truck to disappear from sight forever.

'*My name – !*' bellowed the woman, and the crowd hushed, tittering softly. Paul opened his eyes. He was on his back again. The policeman stood over him, mouth agape, pencil poised. The woman's puffy face was sequined with sweat. Paul wondered what she'd been doing while he wasn't watching. 'My name, officer, is Grundy.'

'I beg your pardon?' The policeman, when nervous, had a way of nibbling his moustache with his lowers.

'Mrs Grundy, dear boy, who did you think I was?' She patted policeman's thin cheek, tweaked his nose. 'But you can call me Charity, handsome!' The policeman blushed. She twiddled her index finger in his little moustache. 'Kootchy-kootchy-koo!' There was a roar of laughter from the crowd.

The policeman sneezed. 'Please!' he protested.

Mrs Grundy curtsied and stooped to unzip the officer's fly. 'Hello! Anybody home!'

'*Stop that!*' squeaked the policeman through the thunderous laughter and applause. Strange, thought Paul, how much I'm enjoying this.

'Come out, come out, wherever you are!'

'*The story!*' the policeman insisted through the tumult.

'Story? What – ?'

'This young fellow,' said the policeman, pointing with his pencil. He zipped up, blew his nose. 'Mr, uh, Mr Westerman . . . you said –'

'Mr *Who*?' The woman shook her jowls, perplexed. She frowned down at Paul, then brightened. 'Oh yes! Amory!' She paled, seemed to sicken. Paul, if he could've, would've smiled. 'Good God!' she rasped, as though appalled at what she saw. Then, once more, she took an operatic grip on her breasts and staggered back a step. 'O mortality! O fatal mischief! Done in! A noble man lies stark and stiff! Delenda est Carthago! *Sic transit glans mundi!*'

Gloria, corrected Paul. No, leave it.

'Squashed like a lousy bug!' she cried. 'And at the height of his potency!'

'Now, wait a minute!' the policeman protested.

'The final curtain! The last farewell! The journey's end! Over the hill! The last muster!' Each phrase was answered by a happy shout from the mob. 'Across the river! The way of all flesh! The last roundup!' She sobbed, then ballooned down on him again, tweaked his ear and whispered: ('How's Charity's weetsie snot-kins, enh? Him fall down and bump his little putsy? Mumsy kiss and make well!') And she let him have it on the – well, sort of on the left side of his nose, left cheek, and part of his left eye: one wet enveloping sour blubbering kiss, and this time, sorrily, the policeman did not intervene. He was busy taking notes. Officer, said Paul.

'Hmmm,' the policeman muttered, and wrote. 'G-R-U-N- ah, ahem, Grundig, Grundig -D, yes, D-I-G. Now what did you – ?'

The woman labored clumsily to her feet, plodded over behind the policeman, and squinted over his shoulder at the notes he was taking. 'That's a "Y" there, buster, a "Y." ' She jabbed a stubby ruby-tipped finger at the notebook.

'Grundigy?' asked the policeman in disbelief. 'What kind of a name is that?'

'No, no!' the old woman whined, her grand manner flung to the winds. 'Grundy! Grundy! Without the "-ig," don't you see? You take off your –'

'Oh, *Grundy!* Now I have it!' The policeman scrubbed

the back end of his pencil in the notebook. 'Darned eraser. About shot.' The paper tore. He looked up irritably. 'Can't we just make it Grundig?'

'Grundy,' said the woman coldly.

The policeman ripped the page out of his notebook, rumpled it up angrily, and hurled it to the street. 'All right, gosh damn it all!' he cried in a rage, scribbling: 'Grundy. I have it. Now get on with it, lady!'

'Officer!' sniffed Mrs Grundy, clasping a handkerchief to her throat. 'Remember your place, or I shall have to speak to your superior!' The policeman shrank, blanched, nibbled his lip.

Paul knew what would come. He could read these two like a book. *I'm* the strange one, he thought. He wanted to watch their faces, but his streetlevel view gave him at best a perspective on their underchins. It was their crotches that were prominent. Butts and bellies: the squashed bug's-eye view. And that was strange, too: that he wanted to watch their faces.

The policeman was begging for mercy, wringing his pale hands. There were faint hissing sounds, wriggling out of the crowd like serpents. 'Cut the shit, mac,' Charity Grundy said finally, 'you're overdoing it.' The officer chewed his moustache, stared down at his notebook, abashed. 'You wanna know who this poor clown is, right?' The policeman nodded. 'Okay, are you ready?'

She clasped her bosom again and the crowd grew silent. The police officer held his notebook up, the pencil poised. Mrs Grundy snuffled, looked down at Paul, winced, turned away and wept. 'Officer!' she gasped. *'He was my lover!'*

Halloos and cheers from the crowd, passing to laughter. The policeman started to smile, blinking down at Mrs Grundy's body, but with a twitch of his moustache, he suppressed it.

'We met . . . just one year ago today. O fateful hour!' She smiled bravely, brushing back a tear, her lower lip quivering. Once, her hands clenched woefully before her face, she winked down at Paul. The wink nearly convinced him. Maybe I'm him after all. Why not? 'He was selling seachests, door to door. I can see him now as he was then –' She paused to look down at him as he was now, and wrinkles of revulsion swept over her face. Somehow this brought laughter. She looked away, puckered her mouth and bugged her eyes, shook one hand limply from the wrist. The crowd was really with her.

'Mrs Grundy,' the officer whispered, 'please . . .'

'Yes, there he was, chapfallen and misused, orphaned by the rapacious world, yet pure and undefiled, there: there at my door!' With her baggy arm, flung out, quavering, she indicated the door. 'Bent nearly double under his impossible seachest, perspiration illuminating his manly brow, wounding his eyes, wrinkling his under-shirt –'

'Careful!' cautioned the policeman nervously, glancing up from his notes. He must have filled twenty or thirty pages by now.

'In short, my heart went out to him!' Gesture of heart going out. 'And though – alas! – my need for seachests was limited –'

The spectators somehow discovered something amusing in this and tittered knowingly. Mainly in the way she said it, he supposed. Her story in truth did not bother Paul so much as his own fascination with it. He knew where it would lead, but it didn't matter. In fact, maybe that *was* what fascinated him.

'– I invited him in. Put down that horrid seachest, dear boy, and come in here, I cried, come in to your warm and obedient Charity, love, come in for a cup of tea, come in and rest, rest your pretty little shoulders, your pretty little back, your pretty little . . .' Mrs Grundy paused, smiled with a faint arch of one eyebrow, and the crowd responded with another burst of laughter. 'And it *was* pretty little, okay,' she grumbled, and again they whooped, while she sniggered throatily.

How was it now? he wondered. In fact, he'd been wondering all along.

'And, well, officer, that's what he did, he *did* put down

his seachest – alas! sad to tell, right on my unfortunate cat Rasputin, dozing there in the day's brief sun, God rest his soul, his (again, alas!) somewhat homaloidal soul!'

She had a great audience. They never failed her, nor did they now.

The policeman, who had finally squatted down to write on his knee, now stood and shouted for order. 'Quiet! *Quiet!*' His moustache twitched. 'Can't you see this is a serious matter?' He's the funny one, thought Paul. The crowd thought so, too, for the laughter mounted, then finally died away. 'And . . . and then what happened?' the policeman whispered. But they heard him anyway and screamed with delight, throwing up a new clamor in which could be distinguished several coarse paraphrases of the policeman's question. The officer's pale face flushed. He looked down at Paul with a brief commiserating smile, shrugged his shoulders, fluttering the epaulettes. Paul made a try at a never-mind kind of gesture, but, he supposed, without bringing it off.

'What happened next, you ask, you naughty boy?' Mrs Grundy shook and wriggled. Cheers and whistles. She cupped her plump hands under her breasts and hitched her abundant hips heavily to one side. 'You don't understand,' she told the crowd. 'I only wished to be a mother to the lad.' Hoohahs and catcalls. 'But I had failed to realize, in that fleeting tragic moment when he unburdened himself upon poor Rasputin, how I was wrenching his young and unsullied heart asunder! Oh yes, I know, I know –'

'This is the dumbest story I ever heard,' interrupted the policeman finally, but Mrs Grundy paid him no heed.

'I know I'm old and fat, that I've crossed the Grand Climacteric!' She winked at the crowd's yowls of laughter. 'I know the fragrant flush of first flower is gone forever!' she cried, not letting a good thing go, pressing her wrinkled palms down over the soft swoop of her blimp-sized hips, peeking coyly over one plump shoulder at the shrieking crowd. The policeman stamped his foot, but no one noticed except Paul. 'I know, I know – *yet:* somehow, face to face with little Charity, a primitive unnameable urgency welled up in his untaught loins, his pretty little –'

'*Stop it!*' cried the policeman, right on cue. 'This has gone far enough!'

'And *you* ask what happened next? I shall tell you, officer! For why conceal the truth . . . from *you* of all people?' Though uneasy, the policeman seemed frankly pleased that she had put it this way. 'Yes, without further discourse, he buried his pretty little head in my bosom –' (Paul felt a distressing sense of suffocation,

though perhaps it had been with him all the while) ' –
and he tumbled me there, yes he did, there on the front
porch alongside his seachest and my dying Rasputin,
there in the sunlight, before God, before the neighbors,
before Mr Dunlevy the mailman who is hard of hearing, before the children from down the block passing on
their shiny little –'

'Crazy goddamn fool he just walk right out in fronta
me no respect just burstin for a bustin!' said a familiar
voice.

Mrs Grundy's broad face, now streaked with tears
and mottled with a tense pink flush, glowered. There
was a long and difficult silence. Then she narrowed her
eyes, smiled faintly, squared her shoulders, touched a
handkerchief to her eye, plunged the handkerchief back
down her bosom, and resumed: ' – Before, in short, the
whole itchy eyes-agog world, a coupling unequaled in
the history of Western concupiscence!' Some vigorous
applause, which she acknowledged. 'Assaulted, but – yes,
I confess it – assaulted, but *aglow,* I reminded him of –'

'Boy I seen punchies in my sweet time but this cookie
takes the cake God bless the laboring classes I say and
preserve us from the humble freak!'

Swiveling his wearying gaze hard right, Paul could
see the truckdriver waggling his huge head at the crowd.
Mrs Grundy padded heavily over to him, the back of

her thick neck reddening, swung her purse in a great swift arc, but the truckdriver recoiled into his cab, laughing with a taunting cackle. Then, almost in the same instant, he poked his red-beaked head out again, and rolling his eyes, said: 'Listen lays and gentmens I'm a good Christian by Judy a decent hardworkin fambly man earnin a honest wage and got a dear little woman and seven yearnin younguns all my own seed *a responsible –*'

'*I'll responsible your ass!*' hollered Charity Grundy and let fly with her purse again, but once more the driver ducked nimbly inside, cackling obscenely. The crowd, taking sides, was more hysterical than ever. Cheers were raised and bets taken.

Again the driver's waggling head popped out: '– *man and god –*' he began, but this time Mrs Grundy was waiting for him. Her great lumpish purse caught him square on his bent red nose – *ka-RAACKK!* – and the truckdriver slumped lifelessly over the door of his cab, his stubby little arms dangling limp, reaching just below the top of his head. As best Paul could tell, the tweed cap did not drop off, but since his eyes were cramped with fatigue, he had to stop looking before the truckdriver's head ceased bobbing against the door.

Man and god! he thought. Of course! terrific! What did it mean? Nothing.

The policeman made futile little gestures of interference, but apparently had too much respect for Mrs Grundy's purse to carry them out. That purse was big enough to hold a bowling ball, and maybe it did.

Mrs Grundy, tongue dangling and panting furiously, clapped one hand over her heart and, with the handkerchief, fanned herself with the other. Paul saw sweat dripping down her legs. 'And so – *foo!* – I . . . I – *puf!* – I reminded him of . . . of the – *whee!* – the cup of tea!' she gasped. She paused, swallowed, mopped her brow, sucked in a deep lungful of air, and exhaled it slowly. She cleared her throat. '*And so I reminded him of the cup of tea!*' she roared with a grand sweep of one powerful arm, the old style recovered. There was a general smattering of complimentary applause, which Mrs Grundy acknowledged with a short nod of her head. 'We went inside. The air was heavy with expectation and the unmistakable aroma of catshit. One might almost be pleased that Rasputin had yielded up the spirit –'

'Now just stop it!' cried the policeman. 'This is –'

'I poured some tea, we sang the now famous duet, '¡Ciérrate la bragueta! ¡La bragueta está cerrada!,' I danced for him, he –'

'Enough, I said!' screamed the policeman, his little moustache quivering with indignation. 'This is absurd!'

You're warm, said Paul. But that's not quite it.

'*Absurd?*' cried Charity Grundy, aghast. '*Absurd?* You call my dancing *absurd?*'

'I . . . I didn't say –'

'Grotesque, perhaps, and yes, a bit awesome – but *absurd!*' She grabbed him by the lapels, lifting him off the ground. 'What do you have against dancing, you worm? *What do you have against grace?*'

'P-please! Put me down!'

'Or is it, you don't believe I *can* dance?' She dropped him.

'N-no!' he squeaked, brushing himself off, straightening his epaulettes. 'No! I –'

'Show him! Show him!' chanted the crowd.

The policeman spun on them. 'STOP! IN THE NAME OF THE LAW!' They obeyed. 'This man is injured. He may die. He needs help. It's no joking matter. I ask for your cooperation.' He paused for effect. 'That's better.' The policeman stroked his moustache, preening a bit. 'Now, ahem, is there a doctor present? A doctor, please?'

'Oh, officer, you're cute! You're *very* cute!' said Mrs Grundy on a new tack. The crowd snickered. '*Is there a doctor present?*' she mimicked, '*a doctor, please?*'

'Now just cut it out!' the policeman ordered, glaring angrily across Paul's chest at Mrs Grundy. 'Gosh damn it now, you stop it this instant, or . . . or you'll see what'll happen!'

'Aww, you're *jealous!*' cried Mrs Grundy. 'And of poor little supine Rasputin! Amory, I mean.' The spectators were in great spirits again, total rebellion threatening, and the police officer was at the end of his rope. 'Well, *don't* be jealous, dear boy!' cooed Mrs Grundy. 'Charity tell you a weetsie bitty secret.'

'*Stop!*' sobbed the policeman. Be careful where you step, said Paul below.

Mrs Grundy leaned perilously out over Paul and got a grip on the policeman's ear. He winced, but no longer attempted escape. 'That boy,' she said, '*he humps terrible!*'

It carried out to the crowd and broke it up. It was her big line and she wambled about gloriously, her rouged mouth stretched in a flabby toothless grin, retrieving the pennies that people were pitching (Paul knew about them from being hit by them; one landed on his upper lip, stayed there, emitting that familiar dead smell common to pennies the world over), thrusting her chest forward to catch them in the cleft of her bosom. She shook and, shaking, jangled. She grabbed the policeman's hand and pulled him forward to share a bow with her. The policeman smiled awkwardly, twitching his moustache.

'You asked for a doctor,' said an old but gentle voice.

The crowd noises subsided. Paul opened his eyes and discovered above him a stooped old man in a rumpled gray suit. His hair was shaggy and white, his face dry, lined with age. He wore rimless glasses, carried a black leather bag. He smiled down at Paul, that easy smile of a man who comprehends and assuages pain, then looked back at the policeman. Inexplicably, a wave of terror shook Paul.

'You wanted a doctor,' the old man repeated.

'Yes! *Yes!*' cried the policeman, almost in tears. 'Oh, thank God!'

'I'd rather you thanked the profession,' the doctor said. 'Now what seems to be the problem?'

'Oh, doctor, it's awful!' The policeman twisted the notebook in his hands, fairly destroying it. 'This man has been struck by this truck, or so it would appear, no one seems to know, it's all a terrible mystery, and there is a woman, but now I don't see – ? and I'm not even sure of his name –'

'No matter,' interrupted the doctor with a kindly nod of his old head, 'who he is. He is a man and that, I assure you, is enough for me.'

'Doctor, that's so good of you to say so!' wept the policeman.

I'm in trouble, thought Paul. Oh boy, I'm really in trouble.

'Well, now, let us just see,' said the doctor, crouching down over Paul. He lifted Paul's eyelids with his thumb and peered intently at Paul's eyes; Paul, anxious to assist, rolled them from side to side. 'Just relax, son,' the doctor said. He opened his black bag, rummaged about in it, withdrew a flashlight. Paul was not sure exactly what the doctor did after that, but he seemed to be looking in his ears. I can't move my head, Paul told him, but the doctor only asked: 'Why does he have a penny under his nose?' His manner was not such as to insist upon an answer, and he got none. Gently, expertly, he pried Paul's teeth apart, pinned his tongue down with a wooden depresser, and scrutinized his throat. Paul's head was on fire with pain. 'Ahh, yes,' he mumbled. 'Hum, hum.'

'How . . . how is he, Doctor?' stammered the police-man, his voice muted with dread and respect. 'Will . . . will he . . .?'

The doctor glared scornfully at the officer, then with-drew a stethoscope from his bag. He hooked it in his ears, slipped the disc inside Paul's shirt and listened intently, his old head inclined to one side like a bird listening for worms. Absolute silence now. Paul could hear the doctor breathing, the policeman whimpering softly. He had the vague impression that the doctor tapped his chest a time or two, but if so, he didn't feel it. His head felt better with his mouth closed. 'Hmmm,' said the doctor gravely, 'yes . . .'

'Oh, please! What *is* it, Doctor?' the policeman cried.

'What is it? *What is it?*' shouted the doctor in a sudden burst of rage. 'I'll tell you *what is it!*' He sprang to his feet, nimble for an old man. 'I cannot examine this patient while you're hovering over my shoulder and mewling like a goddamn schoolboy, *that's* what *is it!*'

'B-but I only –' stammered the officer, staggering backwards.

'And how do you expect me to examine a man half buried under a damned truck?' The doctor was in a terrible temper.

'But I –'

'Damn it! I'll but-I you, you idiot, if you don't remove this truck from the scene so that I can determine the true gravity of this man's injuries! *Have I made myself clear?*'

'Y-yes! But . . . but wh-what am I to *do?*' wept the police officer, hands clenched before his mouth. 'I'm only a simple policeman, Doctor, doing my duty before God and count –'

'Simple, you said it!' barked the doctor. 'I *told* you what to do, you God-and-cunt simpleton – *now get moving!*'

God and cunt! Did it again, thought Paul. Now what?

The policeman, chewing wretchedly on the corners of his notebook, stared first at Paul, then at the truck, at the crowd, back at the truck. Paul felt fairly certain now that the letter following the 'K' on the truck's side was an 'I.' 'Shall I . . . shall I pull him out from under – ?' the officer began tentatively, thin chin aquiver.

'*Good God, no!*' stormed the doctor, stamping his foot. 'This man may have a broken neck! Moving him would *kill* him, don't you see that, you sniveling bird-brain? Now, goddamn it, wipe your wretched nose and go wake up your – your accomplice up there, *and I mean right now!* Tell him to back his truck *off* this poor devil!'

'B-back it off – ! But . . . but he'd have to run *over* him again! He –'

'Don't by God run-over-him-again *me*, you blackshirt hireling, *or I'll have your badge!*' screamed the doctor, brandishing his stethoscope.

The policeman hesitated but a moment to glance down at Paul's body, then turned and ran to the front of the truck. 'Hey! Come on, you!' He whacked the driver on the head with his nightstick. Hollow *thunk!* 'Up and at 'em!'

'– DAM THAT BOY WHAT,' cried the truckdriver, rearing up wildly and fluttering his head as though lost, 'HE DO BUT WALK RIGHT INTO ME AND MY POOR OLE

89

TRICK! TRUCK, I MEAN!' The crowd laughed again, first time in a long time, but the doctor stamped his foot and they quieted right down.

'Now, start up that engine, you, right now! I mean it!' ordered the policeman, stroking his moustache. He was getting a little of his old spit and polish back. He slapped the nightstick in his palm two or three times.

Paul felt the pavement under his back quake as the truckdriver started the motor. The white letters above him joggled in their red fields like butterflies. Beyond, the sky's blue had deepened, but white clouds now flowered in it. The skyscrapers had grayed, as though withdrawing information.

The truck's noise smothered the voices, but Paul did overhear the doctor and the policeman occasionally, the doctor ranting, the policeman imploring, something about mass and weight and vectors and direction. It was finally decided to go forward, since there were two sets of wheels up front and only one to the rear (a decent kind of humanism maintaining, after all, thought Paul), but the truckdriver apparently misunderstood, because he backed up anyway, and the middle set of wheels rolled up on top of Paul.

'Stop! STOP!' shrieked the police officer, and the truck motor coughed and died. 'I ordered you to go *forward*, you pighead, not backward!'

The driver popped his head out the window, bulged his ping-pong-ball eyes at the policeman, then waggled his tiny hands in his ears and brayed. The officer took a fast practiced swing at the driver's big head (epaulettes, or no, he had a skill or two), but the driver deftly dodged it. He clapped his runty hands and bobbed back inside the cab.

'What oh *what* shall we ever do *now?*' wailed the officer. The doctor scowled at him with undisguised disgust. Paul felt like he was strangling, but he could locate no specific pain past his neck. 'Dear lord above! There's wheels on each side of him and wheels in the middle!'

'Capital!' the doctor snorted. 'Figure that out by yourself, or somebody help you?'

'You're making fun,' whimpered the officer.

'AND YOU'RE MURDERING THIS MAN!' bellowed the doctor.

The police officer uttered a short anxious cry, then raced to the front of the truck again. Hostility welling in the crowd, Paul could hear it. 'Okay, okay!' cried the officer. 'Back up or go forward, *please*, I don't care, but hurry! HURRY!'

The motor started up again, there was a jarring grind of gears abrading, then slowly   slowly   slowly
            the middle set of wheels backed down off

Paul's body. There was a brief tense interim before the next set climbed up on him, hesitated as a ferris wheel hesitates at the top of its ambit, then sank down off him.

Some time passed.

He opened his eyes.

The truck had backed away, out of sight, out of Paul's limited range of sight anyway. His eyelids weighed closed. He remembered the doctor being huddled over him, shreds of his clothing being peeled away.

Much later, or perhaps not, he opened his eyes once more. The doctor and the policeman were standing over him, some other people too, people he didn't recognize, though he felt somehow he ought to know them. Mrs Grundy, she was there; in fact, it looked for all the world as though she had set up a ticket booth and was charging admission. Some of the people were holding little children up to see, warm faces, tender, compassionate; more or less. Newsmen were taking his picture. 'You'll be famous,' one of them said.

'His goddamn body is like a mulligan stew,' the doctor was telling a reporter.

The policeman shook his head. He was a bit green. 'Do you think – ?'

'Do I think what?' the doctor asked. Then he laughed,

a thin raking old man's laugh. 'You mean, do I think he's going to *die?*' He laughed again. 'Good God, man, you can see for yourself! There's nothing left of him, he's a goddamn gallimaufry, and hardly an appetizing one at that!' He dipped his fingers into Paul, licked them, grimaced. 'Foo!'

'I think we should get a blanket for him,' the policeman said weakly.

'Of course you should!' snapped the doctor, wiping his stained hands on a small white towel he had brought out of his black bag. He peered down through his rimless spectacles at Paul, smiled. 'Still there, eh?' He squatted beside him. 'I'm sorry, son. There's not a damn thing I can do. Well, yes, I suppose I can take this penny off your lip. You've little use for it, eh?' He laughed softly. 'Now, let's see, there's no function for it, is there? No, no, there it is.' The doctor started to pitch it away, then pocketed it instead. The eyes, don't they use them for the eyes? 'Well, that's better, I'm sure. But let's be honest: it doesn't get to the real problem, does it?' Paul's lip tickled where the penny had been. 'No, I'm of all too little use to you there, boy. I can't even prescribe a soporific platitude. Leave that to the goddamn priests, eh? Hee hee hee! Oops, sorry, son! Would you like a priest?'

No thanks, said Paul.

'Can't get it out, eh?' The doctor probed Paul's neck. 'Hmmm. No, obviously not.' He shrugged. 'Just as well. What could you possibly have to say, eh?' He chuckled drily, then looked up at the policeman who still had not left to search out a blanket. 'Don't just stand there, man! Get this lad a priest!' The police officer, clutching his mouth, hurried away, out of Paul's eye-reach. 'I know it's not easy to accept death,' the doctor was saying. He finished wiping his hands, tossed the towel into his black bag, snapped the bag shut. 'We all struggle against it, boy, it's part and parcel of being alive, this brawl, this meaningless gutterfight with death. In fact, let me tell you, son, it's *all* there is to life.' He wagged his finger in punctuation, and ended by pressing the tip of it to Paul's nose. 'That's the secret, *that's* my happy paregoric! Hee hee hee!'

KI, thought Paul. KI and 14. What could it have been? Never know now. One of those things.

'But death begets life, there's *that*, my boy, and don't you ever forget it! Survival and murder are synonyms, son, first flaw of the universe! Hee hee h – oh! Sorry, son! No time for puns! Forget I said it!'

It's okay, said Paul. Listening to the doctor had at least made him forget the tickle on his lip and it was gone.

'New life burgeons out of rot, new mouths consume old organisms, father dies at orgasm, mother dies at birth, only old Dame Mass with her twin dugs of Stuff and Tickle persists, suffering her long slow split into pure light and pure carbon! Hee hee hee! A tender thought! Don't you agree, lad?' The doctor gazed off into space, happily contemplating the process.

I tell you what, said Paul. Let's forget it.

Just then, the policeman returned with a big quilted comforter, and he and the doctor spread it gently over Paul's body, leaving only his face exposed. The people pressed closer to watch.

'Back! *Back!*' shouted the policeman. 'Have you no respect for the dying? *Back, I say!*'

'Oh, come now,' chided the doctor. 'Let them watch if they want to. It hardly matters to this poor fellow, and even if it does, it can't matter for much longer. And it will help keep the flies off him.'

'Well, doctor, if you think . . .' His voice faded away. Paul closed his eyes.

As he lay there among the curious, several odd questions plagued Paul's mind. He knew there was no point to them, but he couldn't rid himself of them. The book, for example: did he have a book? And if he did, what book, and what had happened to it? And what about the stoplight, that lost increment of what men call history, why had no one brought up the matter of the stoplight? And pure carbon he could understand, but as for light: what could its purity consist of? KI. 14. That impression that it had happened before. Yes, these were mysteries, all right. His head ached from them.

People approached Paul from time to time to look under the blanket. Some only peeked, then turned away, while others stayed to poke around, dip their hands in the mutilations. There seemed to be more interest in them now that they were covered. There were some arguments and some occasional horseplay, but the doctor and policeman kept things from getting out of hand. If someone arrogantly ventured a Latin phrase, the doctor always put him down with some toilet-wall barbarism; on the other hand, he reserved his purest, most mellifluous toponymy for small children and young girls. He made several medical appointments with the latter. The police officer, though queasy, stayed nearby. Once, when Paul happened to open his eyes after having had them closed some while, the policeman smiled warmly down on him and said: 'Don't worry, good fellow. I'm still here. Take it as easy as you can. I'll be here to the very end. You can count on me.' Bullshit, thought Paul, though not ungratefully, and he thought he remembered hearing the doctor echo him as he fell off to sleep.

When he awoke, the streets were empty. They had all wearied of it, as he had known they would. It had clouded over, the sky had darkened, it was probably night, and it had begun to rain lightly. He could now see the truck clearly, off to his left. Must have been people in the way before.

MAGIC KISS LIPSTICK

IN

14

DIFFERENT SHADES

Never would have guessed. Only in true life could such things happen.

When he glanced to his right, he was surprised to find an old man sitting near him. Priest, no doubt. He had come after all. . . black hat, long grayish beard, sitting in the puddles now forming in the street, legs crossed. Go on, said Paul, don't suffer on my account, don't wait for me, but the old man remained, silent, drawn, rain glistening on his hat, face, beard, clothes: prosopopoeia of patience. The priest. Yet, something about the clothes: Well, they were in rags. Pieced together and hanging in tatters. The hat, too, now that he noticed. At short intervals, the old man's head would nod, his eyes would cross, his body would tip, he would catch himself with a start, grunt, glance suspiciously about him, then back down at Paul, would finally relax again and recommence the cycle.

Paul's eyes wearied, especially with the rain splashing into them, so he let them fall closed once more. But he began suffering discomforting visions of the old priest, so he opened them again, squinted off to the left, toward the truck. A small dog, wiry and yellow, padded along in the puddles, hair drooping and bunching up with the rain. It sniffed at the tires of the truck, lifted its legs by one of them, sniffed again, padded on. It circled around Paul, apparently not noticing him, but poking its nose at every object, narrowing the distance between them with every circle. It passed close by the old man, snarled, completed another half-circle, and approached Paul from the left. Paul from the left. It stopped near Paul's head – the wet-dog odor was suffocating – and whimpered, licking Paul's face. The old man did nothing, just sat, legs crossed, and passively watched. Of course . . . not a priest at all: an old beggar. Waiting for the clothes when he died. If he still had any. Go ahead and take them now, Paul told him, I don't care. But the beggar only sat and stared. Paul felt a tugging sensation from below, heard the dog growl. His whole body seemed to jerk upwards, sending another hot flash through his neck. The dog's hind feet were planted alongside Paul's head, and now and again the right paw would lose its footing, kick nervously at Paul's face, a buffeting counterpoint to the waves of hot pain behind his throat and eyes. Finally, something gave way. The dog shook water out of its yellow coat, and padded away, a fresh piece of flesh between its jaws. The beggar's eyes crossed, his head dipped to his chest, and he started to topple forward, but again he caught himself, took a deep breath, uncrossed his legs, crossed them again, but the opposite way, reached in his pocket and pulled out an old cigarette butt, molded it between his yellow fingers, put it in his mouth, but did not light it. For an instant, the earth upended again, and Paul found himself hung on the street, a target for the millions of raindarts somebody out in the night was throwing at him. There's nobody out there, he reminded himself, and that set the earth right again. The beggar spat. Paul shielded his eyes from the rain with his lids. He thought he heard other dogs. How much longer must this go on? he wondered. How much longer?

a little history

Penguin Modern Classics were launched in 1961, and have been shaping the reading habits of generations ever since.

The list began with distinctive grey spines and evocative pictorial covers – a look that, after various incarnations, continues to influence their current design – and with books that are still considered landmark classics today.

Penguin Modern Classics have caused scandal and political change, inspired great films and broken down barriers, whether social, sexual or the boundaries of language itself. They remain the most provocative, groundbreaking, exciting and revolutionary works of the last 100 years (or so).

In 2011, on the fiftieth anniversary of the Modern Classics, we're publishing fifty Mini Modern Classics: the very best short fiction by writers ranging from Beckett to Conrad, Nabokov to Saki, Updike to Wodehouse. Though they don't take long to read, they'll stay with you long after you turn the final page.

MODERN CLASSICS
www.penguinclassics.com